AND HER SMILE WILL UNTETHER THE UNIVERSE

GWENDOLYN KISTE

JOURNALSTONE
YOUR LINK TO ARTISTIC TALENT

To Bill,
My beacon in an impossibly gray world.

ACKNOWLEDGMENTS

Horror is where the heart is.

This has been true for me since I was born, and perhaps it was true even before I was properly born. I have never known a time when horror wasn't woven into the fabric of my everyday life. It has been my comfort food, my heartbeat, the one constant, even when all else looked drab and hopeless. If there is anyone to credit for my love of all things macabre, then I'll have to blame my father for reciting me Edgar Allan Poe while I was still in utero (see? I was a horror fan before birth), and to my mother for introducing me to Ray Bradbury's "Homecoming" when I was a strange child of only four. Growing up in a household where Halloween was a sacrosanct occasion and horror movies played on loop year-round was a delight too few children ever know. So many thanks to those parents of mine for raising me right.

A particularly hearty (albeit snide) thank you goes out to a lifetime of naysayers and tormentors who pushed me down and told me to change, to be like them, to be normal. If not for your negative voices, I would not have had the impetus to craft these fourteen tales of outsiders rising up to face the darkness. And keep in mind, bullies of the world: the outsiders will always rise up, and more often than not, we will win.

On the cheerier side of things, I want to give a shout-out to my wonderful beta readers: Scarlett, Matt, Gerri, Brookelynne, Lee, and Michelle. Thank you for offering your time in service of these stories; the stories most certainly appreciate it.

Thank you to Cassy, my cousin by blood and sister by heart. Your inspiration from the time I was old enough to speak has always left me in awe, and the way that you're raising your beautiful daughter Lily to live in wonder (and to love literature) has left me in awe all over again.

And finally, to Bill, the perfect husband and the perfect muse. You are the guiding influence behind my work, all those stories light and gruesome. Especially the gruesome.

AND HER SMILE WILL UNTETHER THE UNIVERSE

CONTENTS

SOMETHING BORROWED, SOMETHING BLUE

A YELLOW BEAK, the shape of a crescent moon, pricks through your abdomen, and you know it's time. Everyone else knows it's time too. The townspeople track your pregnancies, right down to the hour, so when you phone the paramedics, the woman who answers doesn't bother to ask the nature of your emergency.

"They'll be there in three minutes, Mrs. Gardner."

You're not Mrs. Gardner, not anymore, but there's no reason to change your name because these days, you aren't really anyone, and Mrs. Gardner is as good a moniker as any.

In the living room, you unlatch the front door, leaving it open a sliver so the men in white scrubs won't need to break a window to reach you. The overhead lights are already dim. Everything's gossamer here, paper lanterns on exposed bulbs to minimize the glare, all the harshness in the world scrubbed away. Shadow is best for the things that live in your belly. Keeps them calm. Not that calm matters for long. If this one is like the others before, it'll flap its wings, sloughing off your blood like bolts of lace before taking flight into the world. Chances are you'll never meet it. Chances are it doesn't want to meet you.

Inside her gold-plated cage, Matilda spins a melody, the crystalline rhythm of her voice a fervent welcome for the new addition. A bluebird, Matilda was the fourth, and after she escaped your body, you captured her in the kitchen and clipped her wings. That's the only way anything stays with you—if you shackle it to your side.

Sirens wail in the distance and you wonder what the candy-coated surprise in your viscera will be this round. A dove, a crow, a canary—you can't decide as the crescent beak slices through you, and sinuous trails of red map your skin. It's happening faster than usual, which means you might have to perform the delivery yourself. Something rises in your throat and catches there. You double over and gag a feather into cupped hands. Glistening in your palm, the plumage is pure sapphire, possibly from another bluebird. You hope so. Matilda's birth was the easiest so far. One twinge and it was over.

But a new kind of pain, sharp with metallic edges, sears through you, and you know beyond reason this one's not a bluebird. It's something else. Your back arched like an anxious cat on a back alley fencepost, you writhe, and mincing your skin, the bird emerges, one puzzle piece after another. Two speckled eyes, a blue throat, one red wing, one black wing.

When it's free, the creature stands on your frayed body, its mottled feathers ruffled with bits of flesh. The colors, the shape are like no bird you've seen. With eyes like tiger marbles, it turns and examines your face as if it recognizes you, as if it alone knows who you are.

Your heartbeat quickens like the flicker of first love. You want to run, but you're too weak. So you close your eyes, and the world fades away.

The first time your belly swelled, everyone wished you good tidings, and your sisters-in-law threw a handsome soirée in your honor. There were games and streamers and party favors with fat plastic babies tied on with satin bows, and somebody gave you a cake built of yellow cloth diapers. You loved the three-tiered creation so much you preserved it in the corner of the living room where it lingers still, five years later, bathed in thick dollops of dust and petrified bird droppings.

"Boy or girl?" the party guests asked that day, their flushed cheeks and plastered smiles bearing down on you.

"I want to keep it a surprise," you said, but you wished someone would ask you why, so you could tell them of your superstitions—the ones your mother passed on to you, the only inheritance she left behind—and how those superstitions made you certain something was wrong. You never went to the doctor, not for an ultrasound or even a routine checkup, because you knew they'd confirm what you feared.

But your friends didn't ask. You hid in front of them, hid in the open, and they never noticed. Maybe you were always invisible to them, a faded specter among the living, and this was just the first you realized it.

So you drank the pink punch so sweet your teeth ached and you opened the foil-wrapped gifts and you thanked everyone for coming. It was what you were supposed to do. Pretending was the only way you could keep yourself from screaming, crying, begging them to set you free from a life no longer your own.

Your husband tried to make it easier. As a third trimester surprise, he bought you a cottage in the country, a slice of once-verdant land in the middle of a brown forest. Or what was left of a forest. Most of the trees had withered and died, a disease having swept through years ago, but the place possessed a decayed sort of elegance, the frail branches stretched taut overhead like a corps of ballet dancers preparing before a performance.

The sky gleaming indigo, your husband smiled and carried you over the threshold as though you were newlyweds. For weeks, everything indeed felt brand new and shiny like the intricate treasures a magpie collects to construct a nest for its young.

"It's perfect," you said, a bloated Baba Yaga who didn't need to eat children for them to end up in your stomach.

But the world soon lost its luster. You didn't realize it at first, only saw faint hints of it brimming around the edges of your life. It was in the way your husband's gaze darted away from you and your roundness waddling down the hallway and into the kitchen. You weren't shaping up like a soon-to-be mother should. The proportions were wrong, and there were other things too. Like in lieu of pickles and ice cream, you craved seeds. Sunflower, flax, pepitas—it didn't matter. Seeds were all you wanted.

"Are you okay?" your husband asked.

You confessed your fears to him. He laughed and pulled you into his chest.

"Don't worry," he said. "You'll be a wonderful mother."

Though it was summer and the heat hung in the air like thick billows of chiffon, your skin bristled, and you shivered against him, his luminous skin scented with sweet aftershave and the musk of expensive cologne.

"But everybody tells pregnant women they'll make great mothers," you said. "It can't always be true."

Another laugh. "You'll make it true."

But still he wouldn't look at your belly. After a while, you wouldn't look either, not when something rippled beneath the surface or when your morning sickness yielded bits of down instead of stomach acid. You couldn't confide in your husband again. He was the one who wanted the child, and because he was too good for you, his broad-shouldered body and bright-eyed face the envy of everyone who glimpsed him, you feared another confession would be enough to undo the tenuous matrimonial thread that bound you together. He was all things, and you with your hand-me-down dresses and hair like wilted straw were nothing. But he claimed he loved you anyway, and you wanted to believe it, wanted to give him a child to make sure his love never came unknotted.

The labor wasn't like the Lamaze class said it would be. In the living room beneath lights not yet dimmed, you collapsed to your knees and, through lips cracked and dried, you called out for your husband, but he was buried in an upstairs room far from you, and your voice was too slight to retrieve him.

A scream no more than a whisper, and your stomach tore in two. Where there should have been placenta, there were tattered muscles and something else escaping. A child. Your child. Eyes bleary, all you saw was a flash of snow-white feathers, and then darkness.

❁

The living room returns in swirls of silver mist. For a moment, you don't know which birth this is. Perhaps it's only the first, and you dreamt the rest.

You murmur your husband's name but earn no reply. Nothing can salvage him for you now.

From above you, Matilda caws in her cage, and you remember. This is the twelfth birth, and something went wrong. Or went right. Lately, you can't tell one from the other.

The men in white are here, and they crowd closer to you as their medical needles stitch your ragdoll body back together. There's glass on the floor. Even though you left the door open, they must have broken a window anyhow and climbed through to reach you. Thanks to their haphazard entrance, the cloth diaper cake is in ruins. The last remnant of who you were, crumbled into dust like a beheaded Greek statue.

You search the ceiling and walls for the creature that fled your body. "Where did it go?" you ask, struggling to stay conscious.

"Don't worry, ma'am," the men say. "We'll take care of it."

You try to tell them they have no business taking care of anything except your cleaved stomach, but they never listen to what you say. They take a broom from your closet and beat feathers from the plaster. Matilda screams as though she too can feel the pain.

"Please don't," you whisper, but the words dissolve on your lips like a pillar of salt in the sea.

Something thuds to the floor, and you cover your face with both hands. If only Matilda could break free from her cage and pluck out your eyes. Then you couldn't see what they did to your baby.

✹

Your first birth ended up in the columns of weird news sections, and a few intrepid reporters trekked all the way out to the cottage to meet you. But you were too tired to answer their questions, and your husband's face bloomed every shade of crimson, so the gossip item fizzled before it could gain traction. An urban legend, most said, including some of the locals who had stood across the street on the porch of the general store and watched you leave the hospital, your stomach arrayed in butterfly bandages and your complexion as pallid as the dove that clawed its way through your belly. The same dove your husband claimed to have scared through the open front door after he found you bleeding and unconscious on the living room floor.

"Hopefully, it's someplace far away now," he said.

But every morning, as you swept the cottage porch, your gaze remained with the sky.

"Don't worry," your husband said. "It was just a fluke."

But you knew better. The bird was a piece of you. It came from somewhere inside, and when your husband set it free, you lost part of yourself to the firmament.

Everyone pretended they didn't blame you, but it was lies. His golden skin cold to you, your husband refused to lie in your bed, but even without his touch, your stomach swelled again. There was no revelry held in your honor this time. No friends or family dared to come near you.

The only ones brave enough to breach your body were the men in white coats. They X-rayed your belly and pointed to the hollow shape that resided not in your womb but in your guts.

"It would be an outpatient procedure," your husband said on the way home from the doctors' office. "A few snips and gone."

You shrugged and said you'd think about it. He told you he loved you and wanted what was best for you. But you knew it wasn't true. He couldn't love you, not if he didn't love all of you.

He could, however, love another, love her well enough to plant a child with no feathers inside her. Because he was good at make-believe chivalry, he stayed with you to witness the second form rip through your body. A cardinal, its claret feathers matched to the afterbirth that stained your skin. As the paramedics patched you up again, your husband chased the bird out a window, and from the floor of the cottage, you watched through the glass as the shape departed, a single drop against a vast navy sky.

"I hope it found the first one," you said.

Outside, the exposed trees wilted in the wind.

After the paramedics left, your husband stood in the living

room, suitcases quivering in his hands. "You keep the cottage," he said and took everything else.

Later that spring, you read the birth announcement in the local paper. As if to torment you one last time, he named his daughter Ava.

❀

The men pack up their soiled supplies and march like tin soldiers to the door, the same door your husband walked through and never came back.

"We need to take you to the hospital," they say. "They'll suture you better than we can."

You shake your head. Your body heals faster than it should. Maybe it's the scar tissue built up and toughened from a dozen births, or maybe the birds lick you clean before they leave, a parting thank you to the woman who gave them life. Either way, you have no need for a doctor.

Matilda sobs in her cage, but only you can hear her tears. The other creature lies lifeless at your feet.

The men motion to its corpse. "Do you want us to dispose of it?"

"No," you say, "it's my responsibility."

After their hushed sirens depart the driveway, you look to Matilda, and she looks to you, and together you whistle a melody at once familiar and arcane, mournful notes that have lived inside you both and waited for the right moment to escape.

Upon hearing the song, the creature thrashes its black and red wings before lurching to its feet.

You smile and beckon it to your side. It listens to your commands.

It listens though you never speak.

20

A week after your husband left, two men in dark suits appeared at the cottage door, clinging to leather briefcases stuffed with bureaucracy.

"Ma'am, we're here on behalf of the state."

You told them to leave. They didn't listen.

"Your condition is a potential public health hazard."

"What? Like I'm contagious?" You scowled and fidgeted in the doorway.

They examined you through wire-framed glasses and eyes rimmed with red. "We have to look into that possibility," they said. "It will just be a few tests."

You didn't argue. Arguing with men in suits never worked out well for girls like you. They'd pin you down with paper-weights and wait for you to surrender. It was easier to acquiesce.

So they took you to a hospital and stuck you with needles until your stomach bubbled like caramel on a burner and the next child arrived. It was the only birth not at home and the only one you regretted. The men caught the creature with a dark net and without so much as a nod toward you, they exited the delivery room. As the door swung behind them, a wing flapped helplessly inside the nylon cage, and you caught a glimpse of a feather—a perfect gloss of black silk.

One month later, in a neat brown package, the men sent you the ashes along with a one-page printout of the results.

Normal crow specimen. No abnormalities detected.

You cried unabated for weeks. All the births had stolen something from you—your friends, your husband, your peace—but every time before, you comforted yourself that the tiny speck had soared to the sky, toward places you'd never see. The sentimental keepsake was yours, but the government men stole that away too. Now even your grotesque parts belonged to someone else.

On your nightstand in the box they sent you, the gray dust shuddered beneath the glow of a paper lantern. It was all you had left, and though the men gave it to the incinerator after they'd poked and prodded and gutted it, they couldn't annihilate it. Not completely. One dark fleck of feather remained in the corner, a holdout the flames could not touch.

As a kiss goodbye, you pressed the quill to your lips, but the nothing fragment vanished into the air as though it was never there at all.

But it was there. You remembered how that lonely black wing flailed against the net. And because it was part of you, you were there too, hidden away in ash. You were there, and never again would you let them take what was yours.

⁂

The twelfth bird watches you and waits for your command.

Matilda waits too. You open her cage, and she hops on your shoulder.

"It's time," you say to her, and she leans closer and hums you an elegy you've never heard before.

Smiling, you open the door, and the twelfth bird takes flight.

⁂

After the government men sent you the package, you lingered alone in the cottage for months until at last, the tears turned to stone in your eyes. With a careful hand, you poured the ash of your lost child into a silver locket inscribed with the words TRUE LOVE.

That necklace dangled over your heart the day you started a class on bird watching at the local community college. If you were destined to birth different species, you should at least be able to identify them. Beneath flickering fluorescent lights, the other students in the class stared and whispered to each other. They knew who you were—a walking freak show in a faded linen dress. But it didn't bother you.

At a desk with a popup top, you took notes and whistled a songbird tune. Sometimes, the bird in your belly joined in, and she had a beautiful voice, and the duets terrified the others more than anything you could croon on your own, as though the townspeople genuinely believed wings might sprout through your flesh and your mouth might transform to a razor beak that could tear them into bits. This made you smile. As she stirred in your stomach, you learned to love this bird, the fourth one, even though her feathers had a penchant for catching in the back of your throat.

She was born while you dozed one afternoon, the pang of her birth melted into your dreams of falling, always falling. When you woke, you found her in the kitchen, perched on an empty wooden canister labeled PLAIN SUGAR. Thanks to what the class instructor taught you about clipping wings, you tethered her to you and named her Matilda for no reason except that it suited her. She looked like a Matilda. Her birth was so easy you cobbled yourself together again with a sewing needle and a spool of cotton thread.

But you weren't so lucky after that. The next seven births fragmented your body, blood and muscle and intestines like pink tinsel painting the cottage floors. You loathed the paramedics and their glares and their disgust at the tricks you, a strange circus animal, performed, but you needed them if you wanted any chance of surviving.

It became a maddening routine. As you sprawled in a fountain of your own fluids, the paramedics found a broom or a flyswatter and beat your children from the walls. It always injured you anew to see the birds broken before you, even though once the men were gone, you and Matilda would coax the creatures back to you with little songs that revived their trodden bodies. Over and over, you opened the door and tried to follow them, but they always escaped you, delving deeper into the forest where the darkness and the unknown lingered.

But as with all patterns, it couldn't last forever. Like a change in the weather, you and Matilda could feel it in your hollow bones. The bird you'd always wanted was coming. The one that could set you free.

※◯※

Through the dead forest, you follow the speck in the sky. It isn't like the others. It stays within your sight, perching on a barren tree branch whenever you fall behind. You wander for hours, no breadcrumbs behind you, nothing to lead you back to the cottage and the town. But you already know you can't return. That was never your home. You must find your home on your own or walk aimlessly until your legs give out beneath you and your body turns to dust.

The sun dips down to the tops of the tree trunks, and with your mended stomach in spasms, you suddenly fear you'll lose sight of the twelfth bird in the gloom. But nestled on your shoulder, Matilda murmurs in your ear and tells you to keep going. Because you trust her, you listen to what she says.

Just before night sets in, you reach a clearing. There, they wait for you, their beaks pecking at the ground, exhuming grubs. Doves and crows, cardinals and bluebirds, dozens of them, far more than you've given to the world, more birds than you could have birthed in an entire lifetime. Still, they know you. They're all parts of you, the splintered mosaic of your heart that nobody, not your friends or your husband, ever wanted to see.

"I've missed you," you say, and they chirp and chatter in reply.

When the birds have their fill of worms and dirt, they float into the air. They're ghosts like you, creatures of this world and not of this world at the same time. And they're beautiful.

Swaying against you, Matilda nuzzles your cheek as if to say goodbye. Her feathers no longer clipped, she takes flight and joins the others. They circle above you, strung together like pearls on French wire, and you wish you possessed wings so you might yoke yourself to them.

You purse your lips and whistle, a call only they can decipher. They hear your wish, and one after another, return to earth to claim you. But they don't take to the soil. Instead, they open your mouth and force their way down your throat and into your belly, back to the place from which they came. Gagging, you swallow the feathers and the beaks and the talons that rake the insides of your cheeks into ribbons. You taste blood, your blood and theirs, and you taste something else too. Each bird has a different flavor, all of them sweet perfection that melts in your mouth like spun sugar. Rock candy for the doves. Cinnamon discs for the cardinals. Gumdrops for Matilda.

When the sky is empty and the sweetness ebbs away, there's one thing left for you to do, and you know what it is. You open the locket that hangs from your neck and gulp down the dust. Not a trace of honey there. It smacks of antiseptics and chloroform, an acrid tang that blisters your tongue. The agony the third one felt under needles and microscopes becomes your agony now, and you're grateful to share the burden.

United at last, your children stir in your belly. It's their home, and in a way, it's your home too. The desiccated branches shift and contort overhead, and all around you, the forest is convulsing to life.

Through scarred skin, you hear Matilda sing a melody as the birds flap their wings in unison. Any pain they once inflicted inside you is gone, replaced with pure bliss, something far beyond what your husband or the government men or the townspeople could ever understand. This sense of calm like childhood dreams come to fruition is yours and yours alone. You tip your head back to the sky, and the birds carry you there. Together, you soar above the cottage, above the town, above the people who look up and no longer whisper but scream until their throats are raw.

For the first time, you are whole, and the world whirs to life in celebration.

Below you, the trees are all in bloom.

TEN THINGS TO KNOW ABOUT THE TEN QUESTIONS

Respond to the following statements, using a scale of 1 to 5 (1 being "Not at All True" and 5 being "Always or Almost Always True").

1. Something tells me there's another place I belong, a place that's been waiting for me.

✳

THEY SAY GOODBYE. They say it with a strange smile like a kid who overheard a secret. But they don't share what they know. They just walk out the door.

Maybe it's a cabin door. Or an office door. Or a plain screen door in suburbia.

They walk out and they don't come back.

✳

My Uncle Ray's the first in my family to vanish. It happens in the early weeks when the chattering faces on television and the mindless voices online still claim it's some newfangled fad that will taper off like acid-washed jeans or hula hoops did.

I half-bury my face beneath my comforter. "Where did he go?"

"Probably out on a drunk," my dad says and tucks me in as if that's an answer.

But I can't sleep. My parents watch from the doorway as I wrap one corner of my comforter to a bedpost and tie the other end around my waist.

"Nobody can steal me now," I say, my body tottering against the bed frame as though I had spun in one too many circles.

They ignore me when I plead with them to fasten their bed sheets around their waists the same way.

"There's nothing to worry about, Vivienne," they say. "It'll be over soon."

❧

2. No one feels or thinks the way I do.

❧

By the end of the month, over a thousand are missing, and the little white number in the corner of the news reports ticks higher every day.

There aren't bodies. The people simply vanish like soap bubbles. "It's been long enough," my parents say to the other parents during bridge games and over church pews. "They need to do something about it."

I ask who "they" are, but no one tells me. All the adults and even a few kids in my grade keep talking about "them" as though they have the answers.

But they don't have answers. They have questions. Ten questions to predict who'll disappear next.

The news outlets announce the questions with clever headlines like "Ten Things to Know About the Ten Questions" and "Are These Ten Questions the Answer to Our Fears?".

Bright posters appear on every lamppost and grocery store bulletin board. I never see anyone hanging them up. Instead, the glossy images materialize out of the ether as though the world is swallowing people whole and spitting out posters to replace them.

The picture is always the same. A mother clutching her two children, all three solemn like prisoners whose punishment entails posing for a sappy PSA. Beneath them, there's a catchphrase emblazoned in red letters: *Help us help ourselves. Ask your friends and family if they've taken the test.*

I see the sign again and again, but the test isn't what worries me. I'm irked neither of the kids are wearing tethers around their waists.

"Have you completed it yet?" the smiling Sunday school faces ask my mother, and she smiles back and says we have.

I wonder why she lies about it, but I don't question her. She'll only hush me if I do.

"My whole family's safe." Our next-door neighbor leans over the fence. "My wife and I had the lowest scores possible."

I scowl, squirming at my parents' feet. "A low score is good?"

"Sure is," he says. "A ten is perfect."

I want a ten, too. This test sounds easier than learning the periodic table, and I already aced that in the fifth grade.

So on Monday morning when a bubble sheet lands on my school desk, I answer thoughtfully, the tip of my pencil painting shadows over the tiny circles.

I finish first and deem that a good sign.

Before the lunch bell, I'm corralled into a far corner, my books and puffy coat and Hello Kitty backpack overflowing in my arms. Three others join me.

"Maybe we did really well," I say.

We stand there for an hour, though no one tells us why.

"There's a new classroom," the teacher says to us after the others have departed for the cafeteria. "You'll be happier there."

Between her tight, lacquered smile and sweaty face, I know she's lying. But I'm not brave enough to make the accusation. A girl named Tally does it for me.

"If you're sure this new classroom is so great, why doesn't everyone go?" Tally's wide green eyes never blink as she waits for an answer.

"Because you're special," the teacher says, and then I'm sure we're in trouble.

⁂

3. There might be problems in the world, but I want to be here and help fix things.

⁂

The school sends me home with a note. My mother reads it after dinner and passes it to my father. Neither of them look at me. They never look at me again, not closely. They don't want to see what the test sees.

"Those normal people don't know what they're missing." Tally skips to her desk at the front of the cramped classroom. She chooses the seat because the roof leaks on the nearby radiator. The incessant *plink-plunk* on metal crafts a strange tune, and Tally likes to sing along.

"Quiet," says the teacher.

The rest of us obey. In our top floor room, we stare silently at our desks—old desks with scratched wooden tops that open upwards. Mine has an ancient message carved into it: *Julie loves*

30

Johnny 4E.

There are thirty of us transplants, every grade represented in our ranks from sixth—my and Tally's year—through twelfth. We have nothing in common beyond our test scores, but the scores are enough.

Every day, one or two students sob before lunch.

"Quiet," says the teacher.

Usually, the younger kids cry the most, but the older ones break down sometimes. I do too. We all take our turn. All except Tally. She grins and listens to the rain streaming through the roof.

"Plunk-plunk-plunk-plink," she harmonizes.

I peer at her from two rows away. She's there and not there, an unsolvable riddle. Part of me is sure she must live in a castle surrounded by an alligator-laden moat or in a graveyard where she tutors a battalion of ghouls.

I decide to follow her. I'm disappointed to find her home's nothing more than a two-story off-white house at the end of a lane.

She leaves the front door open.

"Do you know how to play jacks?" she asks from the top of the stairs.

I shake my head, and she offers to teach me.

"It's worth knowing," she says.

Tally arranges the game on the landing, and I sneak gazes at her whenever she's not looking.

"Where are your parents?"

"Maybe at work," she says. "Or maybe they've wandered off."

"Wouldn't you miss them?"

"They aren't here even when they're around." She flips the red ball into the air, and the silver metal scatters. "How about your parents?"

"They're around," I say. "They just don't talk much anymore."

Tally giggles. "No one talks much anymore. Not to us."

After I lose at jacks, she shows me her backyard. The barren fields and skyscraper hills go on forever.

We walk until dusk, her naming birds and flowers as we coil through overgrown paths. The words she says are all nonsense, but I memorize every syllable.

When I get home after dark, my parents demand to know where I've been. I tell them I stayed late at school to work on my test scores.

"As long as you're learning something," they say.

I smile and think how Tally's the best teacher in the world.

❈

4. No matter how hard I search, I'll never find other people in this world like me.

❈

The week the number hits a million worldwide, the government sets up a dedicated hotline.

"If you see anything unusual or suspect your family or friends are in trouble" and so on.

Like learning our own phone numbers in kindergarten, the teacher forces us to rehearse the toll-free digits.

Tally recites it wrong every time, her impromptu threes and fives throwing off the whole class.

"Quiet," says the teacher, "or it's detention."

That's a lie. The parents of the other kids in detention would complain if one of us were banished there.

After school, Tally and I listen to the somber voice on the other end of the phone ask, "What have you seen? What do you know?"

She stifles a laugh and hangs up without reporting anything.

We call nearly every day. Mostly, she dials, but sometimes I'm brave enough to press the buttons.

After a while, we rarely get through, and if we do, the hold time is three or four hours.

"A person will be gone for good by then," Tally says, huddling next to me in the corner of her room where no one will discover us.

But the hotline does its job. Neighbors watch neighbors. Smile too wide or say goodbye, even as a joke, and the flashing lights will surround you inside of a minute.

"We're here to help," they'll say before escorting the person somewhere safe.

It happens to my neighbor, the one with the lowest test score. He and his wife are whisked off to a treatment facility for so long the grass grows knee-high in their yard and the mail backs up and the real estate lady comes with a sign, though the place never sells.

Down the block, another neighbor is escorted away but returns a day or two later.

"Everything's fixed now," she says.

But my parents never let me walk too close to her property again.

"Contagion," they say, and like everything else, I believe it.

⁂

5. Even if I wanted to, I could never do or say anything that would upset my family.

⁂

They assume we're depressed. All us kids in the special department must be depressed or anxious or something else, something that would account for us wanting to exit the world.

So the teacher gives us tests. Every day, new tests. New except for one. We always get those same ten questions, the ones that condemned us in the first place, the ones that aren't really questions at all, but just a series of banal statements.

In the morning when we sit at our steel desks with the wooden tops, the bubble sheets might be waiting for us.

"Quickly now," the teacher says. "Don't overthink it. Just give your honest responses."

Or maybe the test will be there after lunch or between other "How are you feeling today?" assessments. As if they can sneak the ten questions past us.

"Like we haven't already memorized every word," Tally says as she squeezes my hand across the aisle. I move my seat from the third row to the first, so I'll be closer to her. No one cares where I sit, not the teacher or the other students. Only Tally notices. But that's the only person I care about.

On the worst days, the questions are the last thing we do, the last thing we see. Those nights, the test swirls through my mind while I sleep.

I dream of marking the right answers. But not Tally. She'll never color the correct circles. She'll score a fifty—the worst number—and she'll laugh and I'll laugh too. Because if anything's contagious in that town, it's her.

By the end of eighth grade, three students have disappeared, none of them from our class. For two years, we've all stayed put while the rest of the world vanishes.

"You got it backwards," Tally says before singing along to the leak in the roof.

"Plink-plunk," she croons. "Plunk-plink."

6. Things just go on and on in life without much purpose or direction.

On the first day back after Christmas freshman year, our teacher doesn't return. The police search her house. Everything's there as it should be. Everything except her.

"I hope wherever she is, she's happy," Tally says.

Though my parents never met my teacher, they're red in the face once she's gone.

"How can you expect to help our daughter if you hire deviants to teach her?"

Deviants. That's the word for people who vanish.

Other red-faced mothers and fathers agree. They gather in the school auditorium on a Monday night for a performance with twice the melodrama of anything the theatre students have presented there.

Halfway through Act Two, Tally sneaks in the back.

"Where are your parents?" I whisper, but she pulls me into the half-lit hallway without answering.

I still haven't seen her mom and dad, and I wish she'd at least lie and say they work strange hours. But Tally doesn't lie, not even when she should.

She leads me down the stairs into the library basement. My sneakers graze Salinger paperbacks and hardcover Tolstoys on the musty bottom shelves.

"There are books about it, you know."

I squint at her through the dark aisles. "Books about what?"

"The others who disappeared," Tally says. "It's always happened. It just wasn't as common before. But the world's speeding faster now. Maybe the disappearances have to keep up."

She pulls a text from a gray corner and deposits it in my arms. "Look for yourself."

There they are on yellowed pages: the names of those who vanished. And the years, too. 1910. 1845. 1944. 2001. One or two come back. Most don't. They're gone as if the world made a mistake in coughing them up and needed some way to remedy it.

Tally and I sit cross-legged on the mottled carpet and gawk at maps and drawings. Roanoke Colony is our favorite.

"Mass disappearances are fun," she says. "It's like everyone's in sync with each other."

The skin on both my arms bristles. "But they're not in sync with the world," I say.

"Maybe they are." Tally smiles. "Maybe it's everyone left behind that's wrong."

�֎֎

7. The thought of never seeing my family again is unpleasant, but I could live with it.

✖֎

Tally turns sixteen a week before I do. There are no sweet sixteen birthday parties since we have no friends except each other. No driver's exams since the state doesn't trust us with a license.

"Fools," Tally says. "It's not like we'll take the car with us if we disappear."

But we learn to drive anyhow, teaching each other with her parents' silver sedan that has dust and grime and dead wasps on the dashboard until we wipe it clean.

The unkempt trails behind her house become our crash course.

"Is this all there is to the world?" I ask.

"There can be more," she says, taking the wheel.

We borrow the car over spring break. "Borrow" is the word Tally uses, but we both know it's stealing, or would be stealing if her parents were around to complain.

North Carolina on Route 64. We never discuss where we're

going. But the silence we share between us spoils the surprise.

The silver sedan ricochets from Manns Harbor to Roanoke Island across the Virginia Dare Memorial Bridge.

The library book has a sketch of her as a baby—the first settler born in America. The first child fizzled into nothingness.

I tremble. "Poor little Virginia Dare."

"At least people remember her," Tally says. "She wasn't lost and forgotten."

Tally and I and the ghost of Virginia wander the beach, the ocean salt burning my nose as if I'm breathing fire.

We pretend we're Sir Walter Raleigh back to claim his colony.

"Where ever could they have gone?" Tally stands tall and puffs out her chest. "They must be here somewhere."

I laugh and skip alongside her.

We sleep on the shore with seaweed blankets and pale sand pillows. Tally uses a seashell for an alarm clock.

At home, my parents greet us with a search party half the size of the town.

Tally's family isn't there. And now everyone knows why.

8. I prefer to be alone rather than with other people.

So she can't disappear, Tally's foster family locks her in a room with one window. She pries it open.

The hills behind her old house wait patiently for us, and last year's leaves crackle beneath our feet.

"How did you pay the bills?" I ask.

"My parents owned the place, so it was just property taxes and utilities," Tally says, shrugging. "And they had a decent savings account. It wasn't so hard."

I stop, my feet sinking in the mud. "Not so hard? Tally, you've been on your own for years."

"No, I haven't," she says and wraps her hand around mine.

She leads us back to the main road, past the "For Sale" sign in her front yard.

Under the auspices of helping Tally with the transition, the state puts the house on the market. The officials promise to give her the money since the property is rightfully hers, but as the child of deviants and a would-be deviant herself, she doesn't expect much.

"Besides, nobody will buy it." She kicks the sign as we pass.

Tally returns that night to a lecture from her foster parents. When that doesn't work, they paint her one window shut. I visit anyway, crouching against the cold siding, knee-deep in mulch. She and I play tic-tac-toe through the glass, exhaling warm breath on each side and matching our lines through the double panes.

She always wins. Sometimes, I let her win because it makes her smile.

Then I smile, too.

❀

9. It doesn't matter what the facts say; there are some things I just know.

❀

On Tally's eighteenth birthday, we skip school and break the seal on the front door of her old house. Tally was right: the place never did sell. It's too poisoned for any respectable family to buy. Everyone knows you can't get the stench of deviant out of the wallpaper.

We forage through cupboards and unearth one can of ravioli that hasn't expired.

"To the birthday girl," I say, raising the dismal meal to the air.

Tally assembles a game of jacks on the landing.

"Things will be better now," I say, dabbing dust from the railing. "We'll live here together where no one can find us."

She grips the pointed silver baubles in her hand. "I wish that were true."

I gulp air. "Tally?"

"I'm leaving," she says, her gaze never faltering from the red ball and its army of shiny soldiers. "My foster family set it up. They've already got the treatment facility picked out."

The ravioli forces its way back up my throat. "When will I see you?"

"I'm sorry," she says.

We abandon the game before it's done.

As her birthday gift, Tally asks to take a walk at dusk. Our last walk, she calls it.

"I've known people who return from treatment after a week," I say, sinking into the mud, sinking, always sinking.

"And some never come back." She grasps my hand so tight it throbs. "You know which one I'll be."

The leaves crunch beneath our feet. They might well be the same leaves from our walks years ago. Nothing out there ever changes. Nothing except us.

I start to say something, but a gust of wind cuts between our bodies.

"Do you hear that?" Tally stops, her fingers releasing mine. "It's calling to us."

I struggle to catch my breath, the breeze hazy in my lungs. "What's calling us?"

Tally's running up the hill before I can pull her back.

"Hurry!" She screams and giggles and falls over her own feet but hoists herself up again and keeps going.

We reach a clearing where she hesitates, her head tipped back, taking in the sky.

"Goodbye, Vivienne," she says, smiling.

It's nothing like I think it will be. There are no bright lights. One moment, she's there. The next, she fades out like a song at the end of a record. I can still see her for a while, even as the shape of her body becomes more indistinct, the colors of her eyes, her clothes, her skin bleeding together like a kid's water-color palate left on the blazing summer sidewalk.

That heart-shaped face and wide smile are the last to go. I reach out, hoping to tether myself to her, so I don't lose her forever, but my hand searches the darkness, wildly.

Tally's gone. And she won't return.

⚜

10. The world and everything in it never get better; things only get worse.

⚜

In class, I sit next to her empty desk. The ceiling still drips, but she's not there to sing.

The school holds another meeting. I loiter alone in a back corner while my parents lead the discussion at the front.

"You had that girl in the program for years," they say. "And you still couldn't help her. You haven't helped any of the students, have you?"

The administrators sputter and stammer and then say nothing at all.

No one cares about Tally until it's too late. But too late is better than never.

I'm in the last class that graduates before the special department's dismantled. Slowly, all the other programs across the nation follow suit. They have their own reasons—budget cuts, low attendance—but I prefer to think even when an elementary school in rural Wyoming tosses its last ten-question bubble sheet in the trash, Tally's there, stifling a giggle over what she's done.

Just before donning a cap and gown, I take the test for the last time.

By then, I've learned how to lie, which earns me a perfect score of ten.

It doesn't feel as sweet as I'd hoped.

❧

Add up your response, reverse scoring items 3 and 5.

❧

People never stop vanishing. A hundred more evaporate each week, abandoning the rusted playgrounds and jogging paths and little houses nestled on pretty little streets. The government imposes curfews, but it doesn't help. If people want to disappear, they'll disappear.

I finish high school and move home. But not my home. Tally's home. She leaves me everything she owns along with a note in the will: See you soon.

I move into her bedroom and pretend she's there. Her misty form darts behind the dresser or into the hallway as if we're playing a game of hide-and-seek that never ends.

At dusk, I walk the trails behind the house. The clearing where she departed calls to me.

Like a witch at a Sabbath, I reach the center and close my eyes, murmuring the same incantation.

"Tally . . . Tally . . ."

Nothing happens. Not at first. But if I linger long enough,

the trees dance all around me, and her laugh fades like an echo into the night.

I listen to what she says.

I listen, even though it's always the same.

She tells me it's not my time.

Not yet.

I ask her when.

Soon, the wind whispers. *I'll see you soon.*

Smiling, I retreat inside.

On the landing, the game of jacks waits for her, just as she left it.

One more move, and Tally wins.

⚜

Interpreting Test Scores

10-19: You are at low risk of disappearance. Please help us by watching your friends and family. Always report any strange behavior. You are our best hope for stopping this crisis.

20-29: You are at moderate risk of disappearance. Please stay close to your family and friends. Consider seeking professional help at one of our newly designated treatment centers.

30-39: You are at high risk of disappearance. Please locate a treatment center in your area or ask a trusted friend or family member to assist you.

40-50: Call the number at the bottom of this test immediately and share your results.

THE CLAWFOOT REQUIEM

WHEN MY SISTER Savannah set out to do something, she never failed to impress. So on the morning she opened her wrists and emptied what was left of her heart, the bathroom looked less like a butcher block and more like an altar. A dozen lit candles decorated the sink. Opened to Corinthians, a withered King James Bible sat on the floor next to the tub. And with her favorite shade of lipstick—a drugstore brand named Rose Petal—Savannah inscribed a final message on the mirror: *Now we know for certain where I'm going.*

Despite the impediments in both utensil and surface, even a calligrapher would have envied the flawless penmanship.

As her only roommate, I was the one to discover her. At first, it seemed the most natural thing in the world as if I intuited the moment would someday arrive. I watched her for a long time, memorizing the quiet expression across her face.

Then the invaders came. With their loud sirens and sweating brows, they descended upon on our red brick house, vultures that fed not on the flesh but on the sorrow. One man waited in the white vehicle while two others defied the threshold yet offered no words of comfort. Instead, they hoisted her from the scarlet water, deposited her on a makeshift bed, and hauled her outside like a leaking bag of garbage.

"Which funeral home?" The man closed the door to the ambulance, and I realized I had followed Savannah as far as I could go.

"I didn't know there was a choice."

"You can use Lassiter's. They're downtown. Or Solenski's. They're about two miles from here." A fly landed on his forehead and drank from a bead of perspiration. He swatted it, scratched the spot it sullied, and continued. "Or you could use McMiller's. But almost nobody goes there."

"The first one," I said.

The insect revisited his face and imbibed a second time.

The man persisted with his diatribe, undeterred when I strolled back to the house and locked the door behind me. I peered out the window until he and his uniformed friends spirited my sister to whatever uncharted sovereignty awaited her. Part of me thought if I didn't see them leave, they'd linger there until the next time I regarded our driveway. *My* driveway. Savannah asserted ownership over nothing now, other than the remnants of herself she left in the bathroom.

I returned to the scene that now lacked its star. Like a stagehand converting a proscenium between acts, I extinguished the candles that had already retreated to wicks and cleaned the mirror of the message I instinctively knew by heart.

After closing the Bible and placing it on the sink, I kneeled before the final piece of Savannah's magnum opus. The air was stifling, yet the stained water undulated in an almost imperceptible current. That was when I understood what Savannah learned while the passion within her faded. This blood defined her. It gave her life and it revoked it. One pint she

44

could have spared. Two or three or maybe even four wouldn't have destroyed her. But this tub—the Victorian blueprint she demanded when our parents remodeled more than a decade before—contained her murder weapon. The spoiled porcelain was an unwitting measuring cup of her life.

And if I drained the blemished water, she too would swirl through the grate.

As though a silent voice commanded me, I sank to the floor, rested my head on the pink and white tiles, and fell asleep.

❧

I held no funeral for Savannah. The prospect of an open casket meant spectators would search for evidence of her wounds. If I selected to bury her in a long-sleeved blouse to obscure the gashes, everyone would know that concealed beneath the cotton was a self-hatred great enough to be a young woman's undoing. But if I arranged for a closed casket, they'd invent scenarios far grislier than the truth.

Our Aunt Adelle, however, insisted on a wake. She told me I would regret it if I failed to honor Savannah. I said she was wrong. She informed me she'd already advertised the occasion in the paper, and it was too late to rescind the notice.

To protect Savannah, I declared the second floor bathroom out of order. The downstairs one would serve better for the occasion anyhow. Just to be sure, I fashioned a sign to make my lie official. I found a piece of paper, but no pen or pencil materialized, so I used the Rose Petal lipstick on the sink.

"My writing's never been as nice as yours," I said to the bathwater as I affixed the notice to the door.

I flicked the light switch and plunged the bathroom—and my sister with it—into darkness. But her soul could see through the gloom. I knew because I could feel her watching me from where I stood in the doorway.

"I'll be back soon," I said. "No one will bother you until then. I promise."

Even if I wanted to discard the blood—which I had no inclination to do—I couldn't touch the water to drain it. That would be akin to putting my fist through her heart.

My aunt arrived early, carving a path of domestic destruction through my home. Every chair from the garage came clanging into the living room. My mother's punch bowl was set free of a quarter inch of grime. The vacuum whirred and whined and then released a rattle of misery and died.

I guarded the upstairs bathroom. My aunt might demand to inspect it for mildew, and I couldn't let her disturb my sister.

A squawk rang up the stairs. "Sabrina, come help me."

"I don't think so," I said.

They tumbled into our home, one after another until the driveway overflowed with rubber and chrome. The familial shell bulged at its seams and the steadfast bricks threatened to shatter from the mortar, but still a dozen more late arrivals swelled into every recess of the house. I was certain that if I opened a hamper or a top shelf cabinet, I'd find a mourner hiding there, eager to offer a corny phrase that was more trope than sympathy.

Most of the people never met my sister. They were patrons of my aunt. From cathedral pews and bingo games, they swarmed to her. They did whatever she said. And on this day, she commanded them to mourn. So they mourned, passing around apologies like churchgoers sharing a collection plate.

"Thank you." Despite a lack of tears, my aunt dabbed her eyes with a floral handkerchief. "At least my sister Gladys didn't live long enough to see her baby go."

I figured she would invoke my mother's name at some point, but she might have had the civility to wait until hour two or three instead of opening with it.

Uninterested in hearing her recount my family's tale of woe, I faced the stairs to ensure no one intruded on Savannah. My sign forbidding entry might not hold the most curious at bay.

As I played sentry on behalf of my beloved, a hand caressed my shoulder.

"I'm so sorry about Savannah," a man whispered.

I stared at his face but could make no sense of his features. The individual components—the chestnut brown eyes, the cleft in the chin, the thick yet colorless eyebrows—signified some passing familiarity but put together, I could discern nothing outside of an ordinary man with an ordinary visage. I recognized him much as one pedestrian recognizes another on a city sidewalk. You've passed each other before, but you don't know where and you don't care to find out.

"Sabrina, are you all right?"

The stranger knew my name. That was never a good sign.

"My sister's dead," I said. "How do you think I am?"

He embraced me. I squirmed.

"Joseph!" My aunt maneuvered me to one side and flung her arms around the man.

Based on his uncomfortable response to her affection, he was apparently in attendance more for my benefit than hers. I wondered if I called him Joseph or Joe. Or maybe we had some pet names for each other like Honey or Peach. My fingers fluttered to my lips, and I suppressed a gag.

Like rubble from a ship, splinters of memories surfaced and submerged, but I endeavored neither to bury nor retrieve them. I knew him. Maybe I loved him. Maybe I didn't. My aunt adored him, and that was enough to make me wary.

Adelle mixed back into the crowd, and the man named Joseph gave me a half smile, the kind that apologizes for your problems yet at the same time insists you cheer up.

"Your aunt's in good spirits… considering."

"She likes to call herself indomitable," I said. My mind ran through a list of adjectives I preferred to call her instead.

A gentleman with a red, creased face shifted through the

door. I almost pilfered my aunt's handkerchief and bestowed it on him. He clearly needed the solace more than she did.

"Who is that?" I asked.

My aunt glanced at the man. "Someone who doesn't belong here."

She glided toward him, a queen arrayed in her blackest couture. A whisper into his ear, and he departed before I could learn his name or anything else about him.

For the next few minutes, the noise in the room fell out like the false bottom on a gravity carnival ride. Mouths dropped up and down and lips pursed and parted, but all the time, I wished to hear Savannah, see Savannah, even just sit next to the bathtub sheltering Savannah.

Much to my disappointment, sound reemerged in the world. At first, only a few rehearsed words penetrated the air—emissaries to ensure this was indeed the house where they belonged—before the whole, reprehensible din rushed into the spaces where silence had been, threatening to crush me under the weight of make-believe bereavement.

A woman—whose name I may have forgotten or may simply never have known—moved toward me and presented a brief condolence. I focused on the strange geometrical design on the linoleum. If I stared long enough without blinking, the patterns started to move.

"I just met Joseph." She smiled. "What a nice young man. You're very lucky, Sabrina."

"He seems agreeable enough," I said.

Across the room, my so-called lover shook whatever hand outstretched to him.

"Are you two planning to wed soon?"

I examined my fingers. No ring.

"I don't think so," I said.

The woman had no other conversation starters in her arsenal, so we sipped the syrupy potion Adelle had poured into my mother's punchbowl.

After an uneasy interval, she settled on a safer topic. "Where is the restroom?"

I flailed toward the doorway. "Past the kitchen."

An accomplished eavesdropper, my aunt pointed to the stairs. "There are nicer facilities on the second floor."

"No," I said without inflection. "Those facilities are out of order."

The woman excused herself and walked toward the kitchen.

My aunt inhaled. "Do you need a plumber, dear?"

I shook my head.

"Then what's the problem?"

"My sister's dead."

"I meant about the bathroom."

"So did I."

I retired to the room my father called his study back when he could declare things his own. The door closed behind me. At last, I was alone.

But not alone. On my father's dusty desk—a shrine my mother left just as it looked the morning his heart avowed no more—I found a necklace belonging to my sister. I lifted the piece of jewelry to the window as though the movement could somehow reveal what the silver chain and charm were doing so far adrift. Savannah had worn the necklace only a week before, so it hadn't sat in the airless room for seven years. But why she bothered to visit our father's study defied my understanding. I shoved the trinket deep in my pocket and decided to return it to its owner later that evening. Then I searched each crevice for an answer.

The Bible.

There it sat in its rightful place on the bookshelf. That was why my sister had come into this room. But I had no recollection of returning it. If someone had asked me where our family's Bible resided, I would have guessed the decrepit text remained on the sink upstairs. Still, I supposed it was my work. Savannah was in no condition to replace it.

My fingers fumbled to her last selection. Page 686. Or 687. I couldn't tell which passage between Corinthians chapters two to six inspired her. But something there proved the final words on my sister's mind, and I wanted to decipher the secret.

The murmur of mourners pierced the room, and I glanced to the now opened door. Joseph loitered at the threshold of the study.

"Is there anything I can do?" He was the first person I believed all day.

I smoothed the crackling, thin pages. "Why do you think she chose Corinthians?"

He secured the barrier behind him and sealed out the invaders' whispers. "First or Second?"

"I forgot there were two." I glimpsed the top of the page. "First Corinthians."

With one hand lightly stroking my back, he examined the Bible. "Maybe there's no reason. Maybe she just opened it and left it there."

I looked at him. "Do you know who that man was? The one my aunt sent away?"

"I'd never seen him before."

"He knew Savannah," I said. "He was so upset he must have."

Joseph nodded but said nothing else. Together, we squinted at the printed verse and tried to interpret the hidden signs my sister left behind.

⁂

After the wake, I hoped I would be alone. Yet once the funeral guests departed, more visitors arrived, and their stay came with no clear expiration. I first heard their gossips three days after

Savannah's exodus. Roused from my sleep on the cold tiles, I peered over the edge of the bathtub and caught them in the midst of defiling her. I reached to protect my sister, but the creatures proved too quick for any perfunctory attack. And though they knocked at no door, I should have expected them. They manifested anywhere death resided, but I wondered how they learned about hers. Perhaps even flies read obituaries.

I should have viewed them as minor nuisances. After all, the bathroom accommodated a postmortem cistern, so like a bevy of pallbearers, the scavengers had a function to fulfill. But with each quaff of decay, the pests stole an iota of my sister. Again and again, they came to the tub to drink the ambrosia, and I realized given enough time, they'd whisk off her blood like the men in the ambulance had abducted her body.

I found a swatter and obliterated as many of the ghouls as I could. But what to do with the carapaces? For every fly that took a piece of Savannah, the tiny corpse retained a fragment of her soul. I supposed I could collect the leftovers—in a jar perhaps, next to the tub where Savannah had deposited the Bible—but the thought of assembling their crushed bodies nauseated me.

I erased the unexpected massacre from the bathroom and apologized to my sister for sacrificing part of her essence in the process. As recompense, I promised to buy a couple strips of fly paper.

"That might catch them before they get to you." I hoped the consolation might appeal to her, but that familiar honeyed voice provided no opinion either way. Stoic and still, I regarded the claret water until my eyes could no longer focus on its maddening homogeny.

Over the next week, the days assumed a pattern. Purge the room of its unwanted visitors. Adorn our newly adopted bedroom with any stray trinkets I discovered lounging about the house. Answer galling phone calls from Joseph. Listen for my aunt's unannounced raids.

She arrived in grand form each visit. Because my mother gave her a key when we bought the house, Adelle could waltz through the front door any moment of the day and disrupt what little bliss I preserved.

A pile of groceries sprawled onto the counter. Most of what she brought included dairy or soy. I was allergic to both and had been since childhood, but she did her service by bringing an offering of food, and that was all that mattered.

Her grievances opened the morning's dialogue. "I talked to the groundskeeper," she said. "You haven't been to the cemetery yet."

I sat on the landing to keep her from violating the second floor. "Why do I need to visit her grave?"

"Because, dear, that's what you do. That's how people mourn."

"You act like there's only one way to do it."

A faucet somewhere in the house dripped, and I glanced upstairs to ensure it wasn't in Savannah's asylum. Another droplet struck a pan with a metallic thud. The kitchen, I thought. Sighing, I rested my head on the railing.

"I'm worried about you, Sabrina. You should join me for Sunday services. It would be good for your soul."

"I doubt that. But thanks for the offer."

Another drop. Definitely in the kitchen.

"Have you called a plumber yet?"

I shook my head.

"Do you need the number of someone?"

I shook my head again. "Who was that man at the funeral?"

"No one."

"Whoever he was, I think he loved her. An old boyfriend maybe." I hesitated. "Or a new one."

"Who can be certain about anything when it comes to your sister?" My aunt drifted toward the downstairs bathroom.

"She was a ghost even when she was alive."

The door locked behind her, sealing out any truth I might glean about the unknown gentleman.

But in that moment, something else transfixed me. On the counter sat my aunt's keys. Glinting back at me was the one that unlocked my front door. I crept closer and listened to her movement in the adjacent room. Knowing Adelle, she would skulk in front of the mirror and admire herself for another minute. Without a sound, my fingers slipped the teethed silver around a series of scuffed grocery store cards and pressed the furtive treasure against my palm.

She appeared in the doorway. "I'll stop by again next week, so let me know if there's anything you need by Wednesday."

I nodded. Even if I provided her a detailed list, she would deliver the same dozen items she had brought us every week since our parents died.

The key ring swayed in her hand, and I self-congratulated my cunning. But when we reached the door, she halted. Her wide eyes examined me, and I was certain I'd been caught.

Instead, she crinkled her nose. "You should get that bathroom fixed sooner than later. I can smell it backing up."

Another drop against the pan.

After waving farewell to Adelle, I retreated to the kitchen and adjusted the cold knob on the faucet. The water seized in the pipes.

At eight that night, Joseph phoned. He talked about us going on some silly vacation. Something about me needing to get away for a while. All I wanted to discuss was the man my aunt wouldn't mention.

"Maybe he broke it off with Savannah. Maybe he's the reason she killed herself." I paced the perimeter of the kitchen, dodging leftover chairs from the wake.

"Sabrina, the reason your sister killed herself was because she was despondent."

I remained silent, curious what other drivel he might spew.

"You could search through the names of everyone she ever met," he said, "but that isn't going to bring her back. Or excuse her for abandoning you."

"She didn't abandon me," I said and hung up the phone.

On the counter, next to a block of orange cheese that needed no refrigeration, was a lone Mason jar. It was surplus from three weeks earlier when my sister and I preserved a bundle of fresh tomatoes from our garden. The rabbits and groundhogs probably thanked me for forsaking our rows of corn and pumpkins since Savannah died. At least someone was eating well.

The clear jar reflected against the overhead light.

Twenty-five cans. No matter what fruit or vegetable was in season, we preserved exactly twenty-five cans. But Savannah always prepared an extra jar.

"A failsafe," she'd say. "In case one breaks in the water."

I curled my hand around the glass and stared through the dust and grime to the other side. Cradling the souvenir, I retired to my newfound bedroom and talked with my sister long into the night. She was an excellent listener.

❧

I feared I couldn't keep her forever. The flies descended upon the bathtub with ever greater frequency as if the first few escapees had alerted the whole of their kin. A despairing aroma overtook the air and obliterated the remnants of jasmine and patchouli Savannah once considered her trademark.

And they'd soon be arriving. For the previous two days, the phone calls and resultant messages plagued me no more, and while I preferred to believe Adelle and Joseph had simply surrendered in unison, it was far more likely they were concocting some devious scheme together.

To prepare for one final invasion, I crossed the invisible border between the upstairs hallway and the kingdom my sister built in a twelve by ten space. Until then, I hadn't dared to disrespect it. But Savannah asked me to go there. And I couldn't ignore her wishes.

An hour later, they appeared. My aunt toted a bevy of brown paper bags, and Joseph carried the overflow. She groped at the door for almost a minute, searching in vain for her key. I stood on the other side, reveling in her protest.

Finally, she knocked. As a greeting, she thrust a bag at me.

"Help us with these."

I vacated my usual post at the landing to drudge another grocer's special of anaphylaxis through the door.

With a series of heavy sighs, my aunt unloaded several more blocks of cheese.

Joseph frowned at the loot.

"Aren't you allergic?" He mouthed the words, and I nodded.

But Adelle cared only about her thwarted entrance. "I can't find my key," she said and inspected me. "You don't know anything about that, do you?"

I stared at her, employing as vacant an expression as I could muster.

She sniffed. "What is that disgusting odor?"

Before I could block her, Adelle ascended the stairs. I didn't pursue her. Perhaps if I pretended not to care, she'd conduct a brief search and return to the first floor, filled with nothing more than complaints of my poor domestic skills.

Then I heard her open the bathroom door.

I braced for the inevitable scream while Joseph grinned with an almost endearing innocence.

"Oh my God!"

I sighed.

"Adelle?" Joseph rushed up the stairs, and I followed

placidly behind.

By the time I arrived in the bathroom, they were already gaping at my sister. I parted my lips to tell them she didn't appreciate their gawking when my sometimes lover interrupted.

"Is that—" But the smell recalled the rankest of summertime carrion and inspired Joseph to abandon his question and blot out the stench with his sleeve.

"Savannah," I said to assist him.

My aunt gagged. "This is madness."

She reached toward the plug, but I lunged before she could disturb the water. We toppled to the tile, and I hoped she might strike her head against the edge of the tub, inducing a temporary—or permanent—stupor.

Unfortunately, my gambit simply annoyed her.

"What is wrong with you? Have you lost your mind?"

"Sabrina." Joseph took my arm and helped me to my feet. He tried to cradle my face in his hands, but I pushed him toward the sink and turned to my aunt.

"You won't touch her."

"Her?" She stared at me. "It's dirty bathwater filled with rancid blood. There's no one in there!"

"You can't take her away from me."

I charged, ready to add more red décor to the room, but Joseph caught me midair. He wrapped his arms around my waist as I flailed toward the water, desperate to destroy my aunt before she could hurt Savannah.

"This is for your own good." Adelle speared her fake nails through my sister's core and removed the colorless plug. For a moment, she even permitted the chain of the would-be life preserver to dangle from her fingers, just so I would know the deed was done. My body pulsed forward, but Joseph pinned me against his chest.

The water gurgled as it disappeared.

"She's screaming!" I wept.

My aunt rolled her eyes. "It's only the drain."

In under a minute, my sister had departed.

"Savannah." I panted, swallowing my tears. "Please forgive me."

"She has nothing to forgive you for. She needs to be the one asking for forgiveness."

Joseph adjusted his grip on my now limp body. "Because she committed suicide?"

My aunt fluttered her eyes and moved away from the bathtub. "Because she had too many secrets."

He inched toward her. "Like what?"

Impatient to play Greek chorus, the drain emitted a final rattle.

"The man at the funeral," my aunt said, lowering her voice, "was carrying on with Savannah. His wife told me so." She shrugged. "My niece was a sinner. And I made sure she knew it."

I heaved, remembering the message on the mirror. "Did you happen to mention hell in the conversation?"

"I told her the truth. By having that dalliance, she damned herself." Adelle shrugged. "Simple fact."

As he recognized the murderer sharing the room with us, Joseph shifted his stance, and this time, his grasp around my waist began to slack. "How could you do that?" he asked.

Sensing his waning resolve, my body seized into tight stillness. One calculated thrust would shatter Joseph's bones and free me to eradicate the inhuman thing standing near the sink, acrylic caressing her pancake face.

But the unexpected calm belied my intentions.

"Leave," he said to her. "Now."

She exhaled, one eyebrow lifted. "Or what?"

"Or I'll let her go."

Adelle's gaze flitted from Joseph to me and back again. Her masterfully feigned empathy melted away, and without another word, she exited the room.

When he was certain she had gone, Joseph released me.

I kneeled before the pink stain left in my sister's wake.

"Sabrina," he whispered, "she wasn't in there anymore."

I glared at him. "What do you know of souls? How can you be sure she wasn't there?"

Quivering, he gaped at me, yet his face again assumed the look of a stranger.

My fingers pressed into the porcelain tub, searching the invisible pores for any trace of my sister.

At some point, Joseph vanished. I thought of checking the driveway to ensure he'd gone, but there in the bathroom, I was already alone.

※

A stream of pleading messages coalesced into static.

"Forgive me."

"I was wrong to hold you back."

"I love you, Sabrina."

"Please call me. Please."

I unplugged the archaic answering machine and flung it against the wall. The consequent shards sprang apart like glints from a Fourth of July sparkler.

A week later, Adelle returned to the house and knocked unabated for ten minutes. I cracked the door but left the chain in place.

"I talked to my friend," she said as though she possessed only one acquaintance. "He's a lawyer. He told me I could get power of attorney over you."

I scoffed. "Not without Joseph's testimony. And now he loathes you too."

"I won't go away." She crossed her arms. "I'll keep knocking until you let me in."

"I'll call the sheriff and tell him you're trespassing."

"You wouldn't."

"You're right," I said. "I won't call the police. I'll put you in that bathtub instead."

She stiffened on instinct. "I could have you committed."

"You could try."

Her car departed the driveway, and I waved goodbye.

In the afternoon, my sister called to me. The voice in the bedroom beckoned softly in a lilt no longer her own. In lieu of words, this new Savannah used a singular code of floorboard creaks and white noise purrs that only I could understand.

"Don't worry," I said to assuage her latest fear. "She's gone now. And I don't think she'll come back again."

I moved to the dresser and, with a careful hand, slipped open the top drawer. Tucked between a lacy camisole she hadn't worn since high school and an armory of colorful underwear, Savannah waited inside the leftover Mason jar.

"You were right," I said. "This was the safest place for you."

I positioned Savannah on the nearby vanity and watched as graceful waves rippled through her.

"I'm sorry I couldn't save all of you," I said. "They didn't give me enough time."

My ring finger caressed the glass barricade that estranged us. And for the first time since my sister swapped shells, I smiled.

A motorcycle whirred past the house, and Savannah hummed in reply.

"But we fooled them all," I said. "Didn't we, darling?"

Giggling, Savannah smiled back at me.

ALL THE RED APPLES HAVE WITHERED TO GRAY

ONE BITE IS all it takes. That is—and always has been—the rule.

❧

We discover the first girl in autumn. She's tucked beneath the tallest tree in our orchard, dozing there like a ripened apple toppled to earth.

I'm five years old, and the world is still gossamer and strange, my fragile memories like a soft cake that's not yet risen, so part of me is almost certain that finding a girl one morning, sleeping where she doesn't belong, must be the most ordinary thing for those who have lived long enough.

I plod behind my father as he carries her to the barn. "What happened?"

"A witch, no doubt," he says, but I don't believe him, because he blames witches for everything. A thunderstorm on the day of harvest, dark spots on the flesh of Cortlands and

Braeburns, a splinter in his palm from an apple crate—always the work of a spell, according to him. Yet this blighted land, faded and cruel, seems more like magic has forgotten us entirely. Of the whole village, only our orchard retains a speck of color, and with the crop waning, bushel by bushel, each year, even that won't last.

My father places the girl in a pile of wilted straw, away from the wind and the sun, and she curls up, crumpled and lifeless, like an origami swan crushed beneath a heavy boot. In her knotted hand, she cradles a tiny red apple. There's barely a blemish on the skin. A single taste bewitched her.

"I'll go into the village." My father shrugs on his seam-split jacket. "Whoever she is, her family's probably looking for her."

He hesitates, then adds, "You stay here."

He says it as though I long to be near him, as though we're a proper father and daughter, good and whole, not the broken pieces of something ugly and aching.

I stare at the straw and say nothing. Without so much as a nod goodbye, my father vanishes through the barn doors, and I watch his figure become smaller and smaller on the horizon, folding in on itself until he's gone.

There's one path to the village, and he never ventures off it. It's safest that way. On the border to the north, the shadows of the forest murmur nonsense and stretch taut fingers toward the orchard. There are the trees here populated with blooms and apples, and the trees there that yield only gloom, and a line in between, our property line, that divides one from the other, shelter from the unknown.

"Ignore the forest," my father always says. "Only decay lives there."

As if decay doesn't live here with us too, our conjoined twin that never rests.

When I'm sure my father won't double back, I breathe

deep and edge closer to the girl. She smells of lilacs and lilies, bouquets that no longer blossom on this land. For hours, I sit with her in silence, because I've got nothing to talk about, at least nothing this girl is probably eager to hear. She has plenty of problems of her own. She doesn't need mine.

Though she has one problem I can help with. I ease the apple from her fingers and drop it in the pocket of my gingham apron. If it was indeed poisoned, there's no reason for her to embrace it. I'll keep it for her. I'll protect her, the best I can. Too late is better than not at all.

A sliver of moon crests above us, and its meager light brings my father home. It brings someone else too. A young man arrayed in handsome silks and fine jewels, clearly a stranger to our province, since no one here can afford bread, much less such glittery baubles.

He kneels to the straw and inspects the girl's face.

"She's beautiful," he says, and my flesh prickles as he forces his mouth over hers.

I part my lips to ask if he even knows her, if he ever saw her before this night, but I exhale instead and my words dissolve like a plume of smoke in the chilled air. It would do no good to speak. Little girls don't earn the right to question the wisdom of men. We can smile and blush and nod our heads, but we can't tell them no.

Eyes open, the girl gags, and I wonder whether it's residual poison on her tongue or the taste of his kiss that nauseates her.

He drapes her, still groggy, over his shoulders and declares her his bride. The next day, they make it official at the sagging chapel in the town square.

We never learn where this prince came from. Even after the wedding, the girl's family can't pinpoint his kingdom on a map.

"It's somewhere to the East," they say, and that's precise enough to satisfy them.

The villagers don't search for the witch who soured the

apple. They're busy cooing over satin and white stallions, and tethering rusted tin to the tail-board of the royal carriage.

The young ladies cry because it's all so romantic.

"I want an apple and a prince," they say, and cool themselves with folded fans made of lace, torn and yellowed.

My father's chest expands with feverish zeal like a hot air balloon inflating for exhibition, and I divine the thought turning over in his mind.

This will be wonderful for business.

After the ceremony's over and the villagers scatter like dried rice, I remain on the road, my stomach cramping as though I'm the one who consumed poison.

The apple's still in my apron. I take it home and hide it away.

❦

One by one, the girls find their way to the orchard, and once they start arriving, they never stop, like the tide breaking over the shore.

My father makes quiet deals with the families.

"I'll keep them safe," he says, and the mothers and fathers agree, because they have nothing else. Their faces, all soiled and sunken, are hungry, a hunger that even a month of hearty meals wouldn't satiate. This land has been barren so long that the desperation's in their marrow, deeper than the salt beneath the earth, and they look to us and this orchard and our apples as if their daughters might earn a fate here that doesn't mean starvation.

"How do you know the prince will come?" they ask.

My father flashes them a serpent's smile. "Have faith," he says. "Faith always discerns the believers."

They pay their gold coins, often a lifelong savings, and in our cottage by candlelight, my father counts the money each night, pacing circles like a vulture that dines on the carrion of frail dreams.

By now, it's been five years since the first girl, the one who went east and never returned. We never did find her kingdom, but her family claims they receive a letter each spring.

"She delivered an heir in December," they say, but if you ask them, they can't tell you the child's name or whether it's a boy or girl. They can't tell you if the daughter's happy in matrimony either, but that seems unimportant somehow. She married a prince. What more could a poor village girl desire?

Before the families leave their daughters to our care, they make special requests. They ask for glass coffins where the girls can slumber, but they forget there is no glassmaker in this town, no artisan of any kind. All we can offer is a pile of straw in our barn. A hideous option, but my father's clever. He can spin even an unseemly truth into a gold-plated lie.

"It must be straw," he says. "A prince won't come other-wise."

He never asks if they have hay fever. After they're nestled in beds of fodder, the girls sniffle through hollow dreams, eyes swollen and red welts blossoming like rosebuds on their skin.

"No one will want to kiss them now," I say, and my father hushes me.

Such talk is bad for business. And business is what keeps us alive, keeps porridge in our bowls, keeps the orchard thriving for the young ladies who wear their best dresses and lace tattered ribbons in their hair.

But a few don't skip so merrily to the gallows.

"She's nervous," one mother says, dragging her heart-faced daughter behind her. "That won't affect the magic, will it?"

My father regards the girl, who stares at her threadbare shoes. "Not in the case of such a deserving young princess," he says.

At this, the mother brightens as though she always believed

her progeny was royalty-in-waiting, and at last, someone outside the family has confirmed it.

The girl, however, does not brighten. Her skin blanches the color of bone, and when I peer into her face, it's as though I'm looking through the muscle and sinew to see what's beneath. She's no more than fifteen. Some families hold on to their daughters longer, clutching them with gaunt hands, delaying the inevitable, always hoping a better option might materialize. But in this place where the land is stained gray and the wheat won't flower again, there is nothing better, and the longer you wait, the more the girl loses that freshness in the cheeks.

My father makes a deal, a fair one he calls it, and the mother bids farewell to her child.

Except for this ritual, daughters are rarely allowed to be alone. "It's unsafe," the villagers say and keep them under brass lock and key. Not until after the price of their future is paid like a macabre dowry are they turned loose to pick the perfect apple.

Their first taste of freedom is their last.

Along the manicured trails of the orchard, I tread solemnly behind the girl. This is against the rules, and if my father catches me, my backside will meet a belt. I don't care. Like a ghost, I always follow.

It's only May, a time made for fragile blossoms, not fully bloomed fruit, but that doesn't matter. The magic here grows stronger each season, and even in the biting cold of winter, these trees now flourish with ready apples in all varieties, including ones that never used to grow on this land. There's no blush elsewhere in the village—our property has more than enough for everyone.

After the first girl, we were sure the nearby forest cursed our land, but we need no witchcraft to cast this spell. The apples do the work for us, the poison readymade and choosy. The men can eat any of the varieties—Jonagolds, Golden Delicious, Galas—no problem. It's the girls who take one bite and slumber. They don't get to savor the whole thing. What if the second taste is sweeter than the first? They'll never know.

Sobbing, the reluctant girl closes her eyes, and fumbles blindly for a branch. She chooses her apple—her fate—and succumbs to the dirt. I collapse cross-legged beside her, and the tears streak down my face like wax from a flame. Though she can't hear me, I tell her I'm sorry.

The apple, plump and rosy, droops from her fingers, and I pry it free and preserve it in my pocket.

When my father comes to claim her, his temporary property, I hide behind green leaves the shape of giant hands, always reaching to the sky. This is the edge of the world, and the dark forest unfurls beyond, calling in a voice sweet and clear as a cathedral bell. With fingers buried in both ears, I do my best not to listen. The forest is known for its tricks. That's what the men from the village say. It devours the living like a blackened sea. It devoured my mother—or maybe my mother let herself be devoured—that honeyed evening the summer before the first girl came to us.

I never asked my father why she left. I didn't have to. Her sobs like endless lullabies sang me to sleep in the cradle, and the constellation of bruises on the soft flesh of her arms told me what he did to her. What all men who spin golden lies are capable of doing.

Before dawn, a prince from the south arrives, wearing a black velvet cape and a string of blood-red garnets around his neck. He kisses the girl hard on the mouth, and I'm sure she'll suffocate beneath his weight, but no, she struggles awake, her gaze fixed on the one who owns her now.

"My bride," he says.

This is what they always call the girls. Not beloved or partner or lover, but *bride*. A word that implies something fleeting and young. How many days must be marked on a calendar for a girl to shift from bride to wife? What is the passage of time that transforms her from gleaming and new like a magpie's treasure into old and frayed, a burden to be borne? There must be a moment in which this happens, a moment that cleaves the world in two. Does she feel the change stirring within her, a pregnant storm ready to unleash its havoc? Or does it happen without her knowledge, and she only sees it one morning in the way her prince no longer looks lovingly at the ripe features of her face?

This girl of fifteen does not smile at the altar or wave goodbye from the golden carriage. She simply stares at her shoes, no longer threadbare, but polished and silken, the footwear of royalty. She should be happy. That's what the village believes. Even her family doesn't see the shadow that falls over her eyes like a valance of wayward curls. They let her depart for a castle—a mirage in the distance—and they celebrate when she's gone.

"Spring weddings are so lovely, don't you think?" her mother says, red-faced and laughing, as she drinks the last goblet of mead from a dust-caked bottle the family kept for just this occasion.

All the villagers are here, the chortling fools, and because the enchantment my father sells like bone china is responsible for the marriage, he's guest of honor. That makes me guest of honor too. Every boy asks me to dance, and every boy stomps off cursing when I shake my head, folding and unfolding my ragged hem. I have special clothes, an old dress of my mother's, I'm supposed to wear on days like these, but I cling close to my gingham apron, and when I walk home after the revelry ends, alone since my father's too drunk to stand, the apple feels a little heavier in my pocket.

The men who come to the orchard aren't always princes. Some are dukes or counts or barons. The girls and their families rarely know the difference, so long as the groom has a title and a castle and land.

But sometimes he doesn't have any of those things. There's nothing to stop a pauper from waltzing through the door and kissing the first ruby lips he sees. Because who's going to check his credentials? We can't locate whole kingdoms, let alone account for exact wealth.

"It's your orchard," an angry family says to my father after the daughter is married off to an unemployed blacksmith from the village. "You shouldn't have let that roustabout in there."

"No refunds," my father says.

Every morning, I visit the girls, their wilted bodies resting in neat rows. Not all of them are chosen. We now house a decade's worth of would-be princesses. My father has to build a second, then a third barn to accommodate them. Arms crossed over their chests, they doze here, ageless—no laugh lines where they've smiled too long or stitches in their brow where they've frowned too deep. On their faces, there's no roadmap of their lives, because their lives sputtered out too soon.

I say their names as I walk by. It's the only way I can help the world remember. My father doesn't care. He brushes the grime from the curves on their skin and calls it a job well done.

"It's their own fault," he says to me. "They had no faith a prince would appear, so none came for them. Silly girls."

I suddenly wish for a glass coffin, so that I might shatter it and use the jagged shards to open my father's chest and see if he does indeed have anything beating in the cavity where a heart should be. I bet he sports a hollow chasm, and if I screamed into it, my words would echo back to me. That's all he can offer—emptiness. There's certainly no love between us. My devotion, from daughter to father, dried up years ago like the wells in the village that surrender only sand and sorrow. I want to tell him so, tell him how much I hate him, but it's fear that makes me reticent. All I've ever known is fear. Terror of the babbling forest. Dread of what my father would do to me if he could see inside my own heart, how he'd bruise my body like he did my mother's.

I recite the girls' names a little louder to steady myself.

When the day is over and my father retires to the cottage to count and recount his money, I check on the forsaken apples. They live in a splintered crate at the far rim of the property, no more than a yard from the mouth of the forest. It's a good hiding place. Because of his superstitions, my father never ventures that far, always sending me to pull the weeds there.

The crate overflows with rinds and seeds and stems, and while mold should have long ago turned the pieces to dust, the apples are like the girls—decay never touches them.

On the eve of the year's first snowfall, another daughter arrives. Her parents pay with their last silver coins, and my father releases her into the orchard. Stealthy as a mouse, I tag along a few steps behind, but she's not like the others. She searches for no apple. Her eyes looking north, this girl wanders past the trees, past my crate, to the boundary of the here and there.

Faltering for a moment, she glances back at me, and I'm caught under the weight of her stare.

"Are you the one who collects the bodies?"

I fidget in the dirt and shake my head.

"Then why are you here?" she asks.

I have no reason to follow the girls. I can't stop them, can't help them, can't do anything except watch like a strange voyeur as they wither and fall.

"I want to keep them safe," I whisper. "I want them to find true love."

"Love?" The girl tosses her head back and scoffs. "There's none of that here. True love breaks the spell, remember? But look around. The spell is stronger than ever."

She takes a step closer to the forest.

"Please don't." I drift toward her, my arm outstretched, frantic to catch her before she's lost. "You can't be sure what waits in there."

"Sometimes that's better," she says. "It can be freeing."

"It can mean death."

"Maybe." She smiles. "Maybe not."

Like my mother before her, she marches into the trees and does not return. Breathless, I lean against the lowest bough and pray she'll look back again. She never does. Her body dissolves like mist into the darkness.

But she's not gone. I hear giggling just beyond our property line, and her final words stay with me, sinking into my skin like the sweet scent of rose oil.

For the first and only time, the family receives a refund, and I wonder if at last the wind is changing.

⁂

On my twentieth birthday, my father buys me a new dress for my walk in the orchard.

Though the apples have made us the richest family in the province, he's a stingy man, and it's the first gift he's ever given me. While I'm not grateful, not really, it seems rude to disregard the gesture, so I thank him and don the billows of pink chiffon.

"Good luck," he says before retiring to bed. "No doubt your prince will come soon."

My prince. The man who will assume my father's duties once my father is too old to tend the apples himself.

Evening settles softly on the orchard like black tar dripping from the sky, and I take my father's candle to guide me. In the playful shadows, I choose my apple—an Empire, sharp and sweet. I thread it between my fingers, turning it over and over, as though I'll be able to decipher its secrets if only I can see it from the proper angle. Yet there are no secrets here, none worth learning, so I tell myself it's time. My lips move toward the skin. One bite would be enough to sleep deep and cold, like an infant dipped and drowning in black water. My eyes would close, and I could rest.

But it wouldn't last. For once, I believe my father. I'm not the same as the girls left behind. I've seen how the village boys watch me, ravenous wolves sniffing for blood. There is only this orchard, and I am the one to inherit it. I'm already a princess here. And all the boys, licking the sharp points of their glistening teeth, are desperate to become my prince.

The apple sags in my grasp, and doubt, as old as childhood, creeps inside me like a scarab beetle burrowed beneath the flesh. This isn't the only way. This can't be the only way.

The bordering forest calls to me in a voice I recognize, the voice of my mother. My fear melts away, ice in a boiling pot, and the candle as my chaperone, I walk to the edge, a circus performer on a tightrope.

The apple crate lingers still at the border of the forest. With a careful hand, I lower the wick, and the remains of fortunes lost catch in an instant. Though the fire sears my flesh, I clasp the bitten apples and pitch them, one by one, into the treetops of the orchard. These trees are healthy and shouldn't burn, but on this evening, that makes no difference. Every branch is aglow, burning my nose with an acrid scent, the smell of make-believe hope turning to ash.

All around me, my mother's laughing, and the gentle lilt in her voice makes me laugh too, makes me scream out with joy, until my muscles quiver and knees buckle beneath me.

The flames graze the indigo sky, and the light must reach to the heavens, or at least to the village, because I can hear the boys, the greedy ones who were waiting for me to crumble, call out to their families and announce the orchard is burning. I can hear my father too. From the cottage door, he shrieks my name, the only name he remembers, and time slips away from me like grains of sand in an open palm. I must finish now, or I won't finish at all.

This magic is strange. It wasn't wrought by witches, not the kind with cauldrons and capes anyhow. This magic was ours. We longed to escape the colorless land, and the girls bore the weight of that longing. It was easy to shuck it off on them. Girls are always expected to carry an impossible burden in life, like a thousand bushels of apples strapped upon a single back.

In this way, those entombed in straw are my kin. Though not by blood, they are my sisters, and I love them. From the first to the last, I've always loved them. I might be the only one, but one is all it takes to break the spell.

I kiss my fingertips and hold my hand to the sky. The wind carries my love to them, their lips pursed like pale hourglasses. They rouse from heavy dreams, not just the girls here, but those from faraway and forgotten kingdoms too, the princesses and baronesses and countesses who no longer look down in silence and shame. They gaze now to the north, to the unknown, to the trees that cast shadows that aren't so grim anymore.

My mother whispers my name, and smiling, I turn to the waiting forest.

One bite, and the darkness swallows me whole.

THE
MAN
IN THE
AMBRY

D EAR MAN IN the Ambry:
I know you're there. I see your shape in the shadows every morning when I pick out my shoes. Nobody else believes me, but that's okay. In my sixteen years, I've found the best things are the ones you keep to yourself. The little truths about the world that everyone else thinks are crazy. Like when I told my aunt I could taste stars, and she made my parents take me to a doctor. I didn't tell anybody about the stars again, but that didn't make them any less real.

Can you read? I'll slip this letter under your door to find out. You can write back too if you want. I hope you do. I'm bored and could use a friend.

Sincerely,
Molly Jane Richards

※

Dear Man in the Ambry:
This morning, I checked the letter I left you. It was

crumpled in the corner, so you must have read it. Or maybe you thought it was a piece of trash and you were trying to dispose of it.

I searched the whole ambry but couldn't find a letter back to me. Oh well. Maybe you don't think you're much of a Shakespeare and would rather not write back. That's okay. I'll keep leaving these letters so long as you notice them.

Molly Jane

P. S. While in the ambry, I did come across something small and white near the letter. It reminds me of a thin pillar of salt, but pointy too, like a kid's pocketknife. Does it belong to you? I could leave it with my next letter if you want. Or you could come retrieve it yourself. It's in my jewelry box.

Dear Man in the Ambry:

I bet you're wondering what an ambry is. That's what my mom calls the place you live. "Molly Jane, stop hanging out all day in that ambry!" she'll say. But an ambry's just a fancy word for a cabinet or closet.

Do you ever leave there? Nobody's ever seen you in the rest of the house, and I've only caught you in the shadows or when the door's ajar. Are you shy?

I'm sure glad I chose the room next to yours for my bedroom. Otherwise, I don't know how I'd spend my time.

Curiously,

Molly Jane

Dear Man in the Ambry:

How many years have you lived in this house? We've been

here a month, and it's already long enough. Our old place was better. Bigger and with neater windows (stained glass, the whole deal). But according to Mom and Dad, this one's in a better area. A historic neighborhood or something like that.

I'd hoped since it was so old, the house might be haunted, but no such luck. Unless you count. Are you a ghost? I don't think so. Not one chain has rattled in the ambry since we moved in.

Earlier this week, my parents did say they heard something between my bedroom and theirs. Was that you? And in lieu of chains, do you have an accessory you prefer?

More Curiously,

Molly Jane

P.S. I still have your little white trinket in my jewelry box. I'll give it back if you want. No member of the Richards family has ever been called a thief, and I won't start such an unscrupulous tradition now.

※

Dear Man in the Ambry:

Last night, my parents stayed up and listened to some distant scratching. They say it's coming from inside the walls. I didn't hear anything, but my cat Snappy sure did. She's been pawing at the ambry door ever since. And her hearing's not even very good (she's almost 25!), so you must have been pretty busy overnight.

We should play a game. That's what friends do, right? I don't really know for sure. My only friends have been my cousins, and none of them are very nice. They're like default friends, the ones you end up with by accident, not by choice.

But you're my friend by choice. You and Snappy.

I'm not sure what games you play there in the ambry.

Checkers maybe?
Your Devoted Compatriot,
Molly Jane

❀

Dear Man in the Ambry:

Sorry I made you scurry off last night! But you can't roll a soccer ball against my bed at half past two and not expect me to sneak a quick look at where it came from!

I always wanted to see your face. And now I have. Well, half your face anyhow. At least I know you're not a ghost.

And in case you were wondering, I never made the soccer team (thankfully). I only have that ball in there because my parents thought organized sports might be good for me. And what does that mean, organized sports? As opposed to disorganized free-for-all sports?

Anyway, I think it's a good idea for a game. I'll crack the ambry door tonight and wait against the wall. From there, I can send the ball back to you. No peeking. I promise.

Your Athletically Challenged Teammate,
Molly Jane

❀

Dear Man in the Ambry:

My parents are now convinced the house is haunted. "We hear strange rolling noises all night," they say.

Let's please continue our game.
Your Devious One,
Molly Jane

❀

Dear Man in the Ambry:

I should give you a name. How about George? No, that's silly. That reminds me of Lenny and George in *Of Mice and Men*. We read that last year in English class, and I liked the part with the dead mouse. It made me laugh (and think of how Snappy never means to kill mice either), but the scene bothered the other kids. The dead girl was awful though. And everyone just called her "Curley's Wife" like she wasn't worth anything except her husband.

So George is out. Here are some other names I like. Let me know which one you prefer.

Luke   James   Andrew   Christopher

Your Friend in More than Name,
Molly Jane

❦

Dear Andrew:

I found the last letter I wrote you, and Andrew was scratched out. The rest of the names were left alone, so I'm guessing you like Andrew best. Or maybe you like it least, and you were trying to tell me to name you anything other than Andrew. If that's the case, give me some kind of sign. Like rip this letter in half or something.

Eager to Hear from You,
Molly Jane

❦

Dear Andrew:

Last night's letter was in pristine condition, so Andrew it

79

is! I like that name best, too. So distinguished.

This morning, my mom came into my room to discuss school—more about my friends (or lack thereof) than arithmetic homework or anything—and she noticed your white souvenir in my jewelry box. She turned it over and over again in her hand and demanded to know what it was. I said I didn't know. She got all angry and quiet. Then she told my dad. He marched up to my room and tossed your bauble in the trash. I don't know what harm it was doing just sitting in an old box.

So I'm sorry I can't give it back to you. But then again, you had plenty of time to salvage it, so you probably didn't want it anymore.

Apologetically,
Molly Jane

❧

Dear Andrew:

Mom found my letters to you. She claims she was searching for laundry, but I think she was spying on me. That white trinket really bothered her. And judging from her screeching and screaming the moment I exited the school bus yesterday, she would have been happier if she'd discovered a spoon and syringe or a positive pregnancy test in my room. She made my dad pull everything out of the ambry to prove no one's there. (Sorry about the mess.)

Part of me thinks they were hoping for a secret passageway where some neighborhood creeper was living. At least then their little girl wouldn't be crazy. But there was nothing other than a normal old ambry.

I cried most of last night, which is why I didn't leave you a letter sooner. I tried to write a couple versions of this note, but my tears streaked up the pages and my handwriting was such a mess I don't think you could have read it anyhow.

The only way they'd let me keep my bedroom is if I promised not to write you anymore. So I'll leave this note overnight and burn it in the morning.

And don't worry about the fire. Mom will think I'm smoking a joint. Imagine how proud she'll be that her daughter has a normal adolescent vice.

Your Surreptitious Friend,
Molly Jane

❧

Dear Andrew:

I graduate next week. I can't wait to get out of this house, so no one will read my letters except me and you.

College is less than three months away. Will you come visit? I'm going to study psychology. That sounds fun, right? Pedestrian but fun. I'd rather study ghosts and demons and worlds other than my own, but if I wanted that enough, I could move into the ambry with you. Is there available real estate?

No, psychology won't be so bad. My parents said I might finally figure out what's wrong with me. They thought it was funny. I didn't laugh.

Collegiate Bound,
Molly Jane

❧

Dear Andrew:

I saw you again today. Just a glimpse of course, but a good glimpse. Mom was calling upstairs, and all her hollering was distracting me, which is how you must have thought you'd slip by. But when I looked at my mirror, your reflection was there in the fissure of the door. You're beautiful. Or handsome. I

81

should say handsome, even though I mean beautiful.

Did you always look like that, or have you changed to please me?

Swooning (not really),

Molly Jane

❧

Dear Andrew:

Two weeks until college!

I don't think my parents will notice, but you and Snappy will miss me. I'll leave the ambry door open, so you two can commiserate while I'm away.

Homesick Already,

Molly Jane

❧

Dear Andrew:

It's my first Thanksgiving break, and I'm already not sure about school. I live with this girl named Heather. She's got a different idea of fun than me, but then most people don't spend their free time writing to guys who live in the walls of spare rooms.

I hoped you would visit me at college, but the nooks and crannies in the dorm must not be so comfortable.

If you could leave here, would you take the bus? Or would you walk? Or is there some arcane transportation where you're from? Like maybe you ride in the mouth of a dragon or use the fires of the underworld to power a steamship?

Or maybe you walk. You probably walk.

Your Forever Dreamer,

Molly Jane

Dear Andrew:

While I was away at school, my parents converted my bedroom into a guest room. They packed all my things and told me to take the boxes with me to school or else my stuff goes into storage. Welcome home, Molly Jane.

Sorry about them traipsing all over the ambry. But you have a lot more breathing room in there now. Do you breathe? If so, it can't be very comfortable in those stuffy walls.

My parents left my bed (for the benefit of all the elusive guests they must be expecting), so at least I can sleep next to the ambry. But if there wasn't a bed, I'd just sleep inside the ambry. Heck, you'd make a better roommate than Heather.

By the way, Snappy seems livelier than ever. Mom says she disappeared last week for a few days, but they could still hear her meowing. "Like she was in the walls," my mom said.

I knew the two of you would be the best of friends.

Your Faraway Comrade,

Molly Jane

Dear Andrew:

It's Christmas again. The holidays are all eggnog and misery.

Sometimes, my parents still hear strange scratching in the walls. And Snappy's gone. She's been missing for over a month now. But last night, I heard her purring, so it must not be so bad wherever she is. Wherever you are.

Do the stars taste like bliss there? Do you have stars at all?

Your Celestial Body,

Molly Jane

Dear Andrew:

Heather has this trick she taught me. If there's a guy she likes and he's hanging out in the dorm hallway (that's how it is at college, all communal and whatnot), she leaves the door to our room open a little while she changes for bed.

I must confess I tried her ploy last night when I got home for the semester. Sloughed off my academic garb and prepared for the summer all while giving the ambry a front row seat.

You never looked. Maybe you're too much of a gentleman. Or maybe you don't care.

And now I just feel embarrassed about the whole thing.

Your Discomfited Coquette,

Molly Jane

Dear Man in the Ambry:

It's been three semesters since I wrote to you. I guess I don't have much to say. Have you changed? I know I have.

I'm seeing this boy. Derek Adler. He's all right. He says he loves me. Do you think he does? My mom insists he'd make a good husband. We've only been seeing each other for two months, and she's already planning the wedding. A spring ceremony, she says, with pink and ivory as the colors. I don't like pink, and I hate every wretched permutation of white, but May or June is as good a month as any to surrender your freedom, don't you think?

Their Indentured Servant,

Molly Jane

P.S. I found another of those white pillars in the ambry.

Mom says she's gathered up a couple dozen in the last year. She already discarded the others, but I'll keep this one in case you need it back.

❁

Dear Man in the Ambry:

On Sunday, I graduated summa cum laude in psychology. It would have been a good day if Derek hadn't proposed to me over dinner. And both his parents and mine were there, so what was I supposed to do?

Here Comes the Bride,

Molly Jane

❁

Dear Man in the Ambry:

I got married today. People said it was a nice ceremony. They said I wore a beautiful dress.

Derek's waiting in the car while I pick up some things for the honeymoon. Will you be the something borrowed and come with me? I don't want to go alone.

A Brand New Mrs.,

Molly Jane ~~Richards~~ Adler

❁

Dear Man in the Ambry:

Have you ever seen Niagara Falls? Even though it looks like the same Niagara Falls from last week or last year or some centuries-old tintype photograph of a daredevil on a tightrope, it's different. The water's always changing.

People are like that too. I've heard every seven years, we shed each individual cell.

85

If our entire body's changed, are we even the same person? Is Niagara Falls still Niagara Falls?

I don't have many reasons to visit my old bedroom anymore, especially now that I have a new bedroom everyone keeps reminding me about. You probably don't know this, but when you get married, people make it their business to ask about your love life. Like you're an incomparable letdown if there are no swaddling clothes in nine months or less.

Maternally,

Molly Jane

P.S. How's Snappy? Mom and Dad haven't heard her in a while.

❧

Dear Man in the Ambry:

Good news at last! A counseling center hired me. I'll be talking to young kids with so-called behavioral issues (AKA parents like mine). I'm already counseling a girl named Carla. I don't know why her parents think she needs so much help. She seems swell to me.

Do they have jobs where you are? Maybe you work to earn those little white knives, so you can spend them on bigger white knives.

Putting my Degree to Use,

Molly Jane

❧

Dear Man in the Ambry:

Remember the girl I told you about? Carla? Yesterday in our weekly session, she confided in me about someone she knew. Someone no one else could see. He lives in the family's

86

garage. He's like you, only his hair's a different color and he's a little shorter. At least that's what it sounds like from her description.

I'll tell you more when I meet with her again next week. Maybe her friend's a cousin of yours!

Until then,
Molly Jane

⁂

Dear Man in the Ambry:

I'm not counseling Carla anymore. My boss pulled me aside and claimed I was feeding her delusions. Her mother must have complained. Now Carla's with another counselor.

As if anyone else can understand her like I can.

Cosmically Disappointed,
Molly Jane

⁂

Dear Man in the Ambry:

Do they downsize where you are?

Sometimes I've wondered if maybe I wasn't meant for this world. Maybe my job was to taste stars, but everyone got me off-track. I shouldn't complain though. Life's certainly a lot worse for most people. Like Carla's parents. Carla vanished last week, and they can't find her anywhere. I could tell them where she is, but nobody asks my opinion, of course, because they know they wouldn't like what I'd say.

Last night, my mom thought she heard Snappy. But that cat would be over 30 now and couldn't possibly be alive. Especially without any food and water in the walls.

Your Incurable Human,
Mrs. Adler

87

✖✖✖

Dear Man in the Ambry:

Mom called me tonight and demanded I talk to my dad. When I got here, he was taking a sledgehammer to the wall in their bedroom. Something was behind there, and he said he was going to scare it off.

With all that pounding, I sure hope he didn't disturb your rest too much. But don't worry if he did. He's calmer now. "Mice," I told him. "It's only mice."

Are there any pests in the walls? I hope not. How unpleasant that would be for you!

The Not-So-Mousy,

Molly Jane

✖✖✖

Dear Andrew:

After Sunday dinner, I found the gift you left me. It made me laugh. Laugh like a hopeless hysteric until my parents and Derek ran all the way upstairs to check on me. They didn't laugh. I guess a pile of dead mice doesn't have traditional comic appeal. I explained it was an inside joke, but they still didn't laugh. Not even a slight smile. And Derek was so mad he went home without me. Something about needing space. He says he'll pick me up in the morning, but I don't care if he does. What a curmudgeon.

Would you like any rat poison or mouse traps? I could leave some with the next letter.

Yours Truly,

Molly Jane

P.S. I'm still laughing and will be even after I put this letter in the ambry.

P.P.S. Did you like the gift I gave you in return?

§

Dear Man in the Ambry:

Derek has a plan. A plan he thinks will "even out my disposition".

"And you're not working right now," he said. "It's the perfect time."

I bet he thinks a mother could never giggle at a glut of dead rodents.

My parents are already nudging each other and smiling more than usual over meals. Like the three of them are colluding against me. Like they know something I don't.

Doubtfully,
Derek's Wife

§

Dear Man in the Ambry:

I found out what my parents were hiding. They bought a new place closer to me and Derek. Closer for when they have grandkids. As if the offspring are inevitable.

Their last day in this house is in less than two weeks.

I offered to stay and help them pack. But I don't care about packing. I care about writing to you as many times as I can before I never can again.

Your Friend,
Molly Jane

§

Dear Man in the Ambry:

Twelve days until we abandon the house.

I'm not feeling well this evening, so I'll leave it at that.
Hopelessly,
Molly Jane

❧

Dear Man in the Ambry:
Ten days.
I'm still sick, but it comes and goes, so I doubt it's terminal.
My dad keeps saying he's happy we're leaving, especially since the scratching in the walls has started again. Mom wants to leave sooner to appease him, but I begged her to wait. I want every moment I can spend in the ambry.
Please visit me soon. I miss your face. I miss it so much.
Eagerly,
Molly Jane

❧

Dear Man in the Ambry:
Thank you for coming overnight. It was nice to know someone was there, even if I could only hear you breathing.
Four days left. I'm nauseous. And tired. And out of things to tell you except I'm sorry. But I can't stop them. It's their house to sell.
Tenuously,
Molly Jane

❧

Dear Andrew:
I know now why I've been sick. Turns out it is terminal. I'm pregnant.
I tried to be careful. I tried to avoid it. Whichever time

damned me, I'll never know, but I'm damned nonetheless.

Desperately,

Molly Jane

Andrew:

This is the last night here. My parents and Derek are out to dinner. Celebrating the move. I stayed home, said I was sick. And I am sick. I need you to come to me one last time. Before it's too late.

They'll be back soon. I'll put this letter in the ambry, and I'll wait.

Maybe there aren't stars where you are. Maybe Snappy's not there either. Maybe the fires of the underworld will turn me to ash.

But I want the chance to discover that for myself.

For the Last Time,

Molly Jane

P.S. They don't know about me. And I never want them to find out.

To the Man Living in our Former Ambry:

I know you're there. I know because you took my daughter.

At first, we thought Molly Jane just wanted to scare us. We didn't even report it for the first few days because we figured she'd come back.

That was a year ago. The police conducted a search, a pretty exhaustive one I might add, but her father and I couldn't see the point. It was more for her husband's benefit. Did she tell you she was married?

We hired some men to look for you. They pulled out all the walls to see if she was in there. It was like we thought. There's no way in or out of the ambry except the door to her bedroom.

But then the men inspected the walling they'd removed. They all said it was the darndest thing. They said it looked like someone wrote on the back of that paneling. Not words any of us could read. Maybe not words at all. More like something trying to write. Something with claws. Claws like pillars of salt.

Please let her come home. Her husband and parents miss her. She belongs with us.

Sincerely,

A Distraught Mother

P.S. Please stop cooing at night. And stop giggling too. It's scaring the new tenants.

FIND ME, MOMMY

E MMA JO IS good at hide-and-seek.

"Come and find me, Mommy!" she squeals and races down the hall, her pink footie pajamas making hollow thumps on the hardwood floor.

She never plays this game with her father. She only plays with me. I wish I could stop her, but she's out of my reach before I can say a word.

So I follow the sound of giggling.

Her playroom is dim. Even the nightlight in the corner is flicked off.

"Where are you, baby?" I ask the darkness, but the darkness doesn't reply.

I peek under the bed, inside the closet, behind her toy box. She's not here—not at first. Emma Jo doesn't move like other children. She slips into the quiet places I can't see—gaps in the walls and cracks along the ceiling. And where she goes, she's not alone. Something's waiting in those empty spaces for her, a darkness that calls to my daughter in a voice only she can hear.

I check the playroom once, twice, and then I stand in the hall. That's the rule. As long as I play the game right, she'll return to me.

But each time, I wait outside the playroom a little longer. The darkness likes Emma Jo. It doesn't want to give her back.

At last, I hear that giggle of hers, like a crisp wind chime in autumn, and I stumble through the doorway. Emma Jo's behind the toy box, grinning with her crooked milk teeth.

"You found me!" She leaps into my arms, her icy breath as sweet as pink lemonade.

"Next time," I say, "don't go so far, baby. You might not find your way back."

I hug her a little tighter. It's the only way I know she's really here.

⁂

Soon she's not here, the chill of her breath spreading through her body like poison.

Emma Jo no longer runs. She can barely walk, and the doctors can't tell us why.

"Maybe it's a bug," they say.

They run tests, lots of tests, and extract vial after vial of her blood. She cries at the sight of needles and tries to hide. I hold her down to keep her from escaping into the caverns of their stethoscopes. She cries harder. I cry too.

It doesn't help. Each day, my daughter slips a little further from me.

"Why can't you find me, Mommy?" she asks from her hospital bed.

"Where are you, baby?" I cradle her against me while my husband paces the room. He says nothing, does nothing, when the darkness clenches its moonlit fingers around our daughter's throat and steals her from us. That's against the rules of this game, but the darkness doesn't care.

After I put my baby in the earth with pine and lace, I search the house for a keepsake to help me remember her. She left nothing behind. When she was well, Emma Jo was always moving so fast. In pictures, her shape is no more than a blur. A dark blur with a shadow at her side.

"Where did it take her?" I sob, and my husband embraces me. His scent isn't sweet like lemonade. Instead, he stinks of cheap breath mints and cigarette tar and something else, something bitter. His gaze that pleads with me over silent dinners always says the same thing: *We can try again. We can have another child.* As though Emma Jo is gone forever. He doesn't believe me when I tell him she's still hiding somewhere, waiting for me to find her.

"I'm here, Emma Jo," I say to the gloom as my husband shakes his head.

For my birthday, he gives me a painting. It's a rummage sale rendition of an old folktale my grandmother told me when I was young. A woman in a dark veil dragged into a grave by her dead companion.

"She mourned too long," my husband says. "She mourned until something came back."

I toss the picture in the trash and say nothing else. My husband doesn't say anything either. He just tucks his dress shirts in a garment bag and zips his toothbrush in a little black satchel.

His outline lingers in the doorway as if he expects me to ask him to stay. I don't bother looking at him. I'm looking for her.

"Where are you, baby?" I whisper to the walls.

Others offer to help me search. Women with crystal balls and ridiculous names like Madame Zoltair. Their handcrafted signs claim they can reach the other side.

"For a price," they say.

Arrayed in black, I sit in their drooping carnival tents and watch them levitate old wooden tables until they claim they've found her.

They're wrong. Like mist, Emma Jo glides away from them.

"She was right here," they say. "We don't know where she went."

But I know.

At home, her playroom's dark. I check there once, I check twice, and then I stand in the hall and wait until I hear it.

A giggle. That tiny giggle.

"Emma Jo?"

Behind the toy box, there's a shadow where it doesn't belong.

"Mommy?" The voice warbles strangely like the cries of a baby bird that's toppled from its nest.

My lips go dry, and I start to drift backwards—into the hallway, toward the front door, my feet carrying me from this place and whatever's veiled in the gloom.

Then something wafts through the air and stops me. Something familiar.

A sugary aroma like pink lemonade.

I think suddenly of that painting and the twisted expression on the woman's face as the earth devours her. My husband's right. There are things in this world that can return to us. Things so much worse than death.

But none of that is important now. All that matters is Emma Jo is hiding.

And this time, I'm going to find her.

AUDREY
AT
NIGHT

AT HALF PAST midnight, Audrey crawled across the bed-room floor. I couldn't see her at first. But the scratching of fingernails along the carpet as she dragged herself was enough.

Next to me on the mattress, Daniel snored in his usual rhythm. I inspected his hulking figure in the darkness and prayed for him to awaken. But he turned toward the window, still dozing. For five years, he'd slept through her nocturnal cameos.

My gaze returned to the floor. Audrey had reached the edge of the rug. As long as I watched her, she never moved nearer. But if I closed or averted my eyes for a moment, she'd drift a few inches closer to the bed.

I asked her what she wanted, but she never answered.

We stared at each other until sunrise. Then she heaved her body to the doorway and disappeared down the hall.

When Daniel's alarm clock roused him from bed, I was already hunched over the toilet.

"Is there anything I can do?" He stood at the threshold of the bathroom, tightening his tie.

I shook my head and wiped the sweat from my cheeks.

Daniel smiled. "I sometimes think you got pregnant so you could quit work and stay in bed all day."

I retched and thought if Audrey permitted me a night's sleep, I wouldn't have lost my last three jobs.

"I can get your lunch ready for you," I said.

"You need to rest," he said. "And I think I can manage to make a sandwich on my own."

Daniel started for the kitchen, but his steps faltered halfway there. "Kaylee, I asked you before to stop rearranging the furniture. The lifting's not safe for the baby."

I peered into the hallway. "I haven't moved anything."

His calloused fingertips traced the scratch marks in the hardwood floor. "You don't need to lie. Just don't hurt yourself."

"I'm sorry," I said. "It won't happen again."

After another hour of searing nausea, I retreated to the bedroom where my toes straightened the tassels on the rug. Like notches in a tree measuring a child's growth, the fringe helped me gauge Audrey's progress each night. She hadn't made it past the tassels yet, and I hoped she never would.

Alone until late afternoon, I rested on the couch in the living room. While the daytime protected me from Audrey, I couldn't sleep in bed. Fingernails clawed at the hardwood and carpet, even when she wasn't there.

At around three, the phone rang and jolted me from my nap. It was the real estate agent.

"That house on Second Street is back on the market," she said. "The family decided to sell after all. Would you like to enter a bid?"

I rubbed my face and yawned. "We're not looking for a place anymore."

"Mrs. Cooke, I'm sure if we tried again, we could find you

your dream home."

"Not interested," I said and turned off the phone.

After Audrey's debut, I told Daniel I wanted to move. I never said why, and he never asked. Maybe she wouldn't follow, I reasoned to myself. Yet the closing on every house we attempted to buy would falter in the final stage. The owners changed their minds, or the bank refused a loan for which we qualified. Not until a historic Tudor burned to the ground in one of the hottest recorded fires in the history of our little town did I acquiesce to Audrey and agree to stay. Again, Daniel didn't ask why, and I didn't tell him.

He arrived home around six. We ate dinner. He showered. I washed dishes. He read the newspaper. I vomited in the sink.

"I thought morning sickness was supposed to be in the morning," Daniel said as he ambled into the kitchen and wrapped his arms around me.

"Most of the time it is." I wiped my mouth and looked past the red and white curtains. It was dark now. Audrey was on her way.

I dangled my legs over the side of the mattress. "Can we please leave the light on tonight?"

"Baby, it's like I said before." Daniel kicked his slippers to the floor. "I can't sleep when it's bright."

The lamp dimmed, and within a minute, he started to snore.

Audrey crawled on her stomach. She never stood or walked upright. I wondered if death rendered the legs lame or if something else happened to her. Whatever the reason, on most nights, she could barely raise her head. If not for those cerulean eyes flitting back and forth, the body might have been a displaced corpse hunting for a morgue.

Daniel rolled toward me. I leapt over him and smacked the bedside light. In an instant, the room returned to life.

He grabbed me by my waist. "What's wrong?"

I searched the floor. Audrey was gone.

"Nothing," I said.

"You've got to stop this, Kaylee." He kissed my forehead. "I need to sleep."

Plunged once again into darkness, I waited. She lingered in the room. Audrey was a petite thing, five feet tall and no more than ninety pounds. I could search for her, but she might hide. Under the dresser perhaps or along the bed below the baseboard.

After a moment of strained silence, a delicate scratching disturbed the bedroom's stillness, and I looked over the sheets until she materialized, that expressionless face studying my every shudder.

Her ringlet curls poured onto the floor, and the deep red was just as beautiful as I remembered from high school. I always wanted that hair, but she'd laugh and tell me I couldn't have it. So when I was twenty-two, I took something else of hers instead. I married him, and on the day of the wedding, Audrey swallowed a bottle of pills to celebrate the occasion.

"I'm sorry," I whispered through the gloom, though I doubted she cared.

Audrey used to wait weeks between visits, but now she came every night. She came because there was something she wanted.

"You can't have her." I pressed both hands into my abdomen and willed Audrey away.

But the phantom remained. She stared into me, never blinking, until the sunrise arrived and spirited her to whatever bleak domicile received her society each day.

✺✺✺

"Don't leave me here."

Daniel slung his overnight bag across his shoulders.

"Kaylee, someone has to make money. And this trip's been planned for months."

"Let me come with you." I advanced toward him. "I don't feel safe alone."

"Have your mother come stay with you."

I shook my head. I wouldn't let Audrey hurt anyone else I loved.

He stood at the door, a hint of a gut peeking out from his suit jacket. A year after we married, his former football muscles went slack, and fat moved into the places strength used to live. Some days, he was more like a charlatan imitating Daniel. But under the skylight that morning, the face belonged to the man I wed.

I collapsed to the floor and wrapped my arms around his legs. "You're the only thing that protects me!"

"Get up, Kaylee," he said. "You're acting like a child."

"But you're taking the car. I can't even drive anywhere."

"Call your parents. Call my parents if you need a ride." He lifted me to my feet. "Baby, you're going to be fine. This pregnancy has made you crazy."

I ran both hands across my face to dry the tears. "You're right," I said. "I'm sorry. Have a safe trip."

Once Daniel was gone, the presence of Audrey filled his vacancy with glee. Although daylight temporarily tethered her, her soul demanded recompense at all hours, and I wanted to give it to her before she took something else.

With a remote queasiness as my escort, I walked to the cemetery where she was buried. The modest grave was well-manicured, giving no hint of its restless denizen. Her secrets waited elsewhere—in a little gray house nestled among the ranks of slumbering suburbia.

"What do you want?" Audrey's mother grasped the edge of the front door, eager to seal me out if I couldn't invent a reason for intruding.

"Hello, Mrs. Anderson." I gawked at the welcome mat. It was the same one from a decade earlier, back when I was welcomed. "I was hoping we could talk. About Audrey."

Glaring, she beckoned me inside. "You're lucky my husband's at work. You wouldn't make it past the porch light if he was here."

The distant aroma of cinnamon and roses that once permeated the home had long ago faded, and the stench of blue window cleaner and bleach erased any sense of comfort.

"I'm having iced tea." Mrs. Anderson shook her glass and led me into the den. "I'd ask you if you wanted something, but I'd rather see you die of dehydration."

"I'm good anyhow," I said and examined the sterile walls where the family portraits used to hang. There were no pictures of Audrey. The house blotted her from existence. "The place looks different."

"Don't you judge me, Kaylee," she said, tightening her grip on the cup as though she planned to toss the contents into my face. "I removed those photographs because I couldn't stand to see her smile frozen."

"I wasn't judging." I focused on the red grooves of the glass that now rested somberly in her hands.

"When was the last time you were here?" Mrs. Anderson pursed her lips, and I knew she remembered without thinking about it. She waited, testing me to see if I could do the same.

"Audrey's college graduation party."

She smiled. "That's right," she said. "I took the nicest picture of you and Audrey and Daniel that afternoon. It was the last time you were all together."

"That was a good day," I said.

Searching the altered room for a relic from my youth, I found my childhood on a shelf on the wall. It was a kitschy figure, no bigger than a soda can. When we were ten years old, I convinced Audrey to help me get it down, and in our heist, the big-eyed porcelain child toppled to the floor and shattered into pieces. Audrey cried, even after I warned her tears would get us caught, but when Mrs. Anderson found us, she just shook her head and glued the thing back together.

From where I sat, though, I could glimpse the damaged corner where the ceramic lost the smallest shard that she never did find.

"You were a louse of a child," Mrs. Anderson said as if intuiting my thoughts. "You were spoiled. And vain. But my daughter insisted I was wrong about you. So I figured you were a lesson she needed to learn."

She sipped her iced tea as she collected her face—a face that if not for the sorrow etched into every wrinkle would look no different than it had during my heyday with Audrey.

"And she learned about you all right. Put her six feet under, but she learned." Mrs. Anderson smiled a tight smirk. "You always had a penchant for other girls' boyfriends."

I wanted to tell her she was wrong, but I knew she wasn't. Audrey was the last in a line of childhood follies, mistakes for which an adult can never atone.

The clock chimed four in the afternoon, and Mrs. Anderson sighed. "So what do you want, Kaylee?"

"I've been seeing her."

"In your nightmares?"

I shook my head. "She visits me," I said. "When Daniel's sleeping, she comes to the house. Drags herself on the floor in the bedroom."

"Night terrors, Kaylee. That's the clinical name for it. Go to a doctor. They'll fix you up."

"There are marks on the floor where she's been."

Mrs. Anderson laughed, and the single, effervescent burst agitated the wounded figure on its shelf. "Then you need help. Serious psychiatric help."

We sat in silence for several minutes.

"May I use your restroom?"

She waved her hand. "You know where it is."

Scurrying past the bathroom, I proceeded toward the door at the end of the hall. A light was lit within.

Audrey's bedroom wasn't as expected. I figured either Mrs. Anderson converted the space like she did the rest of the house or she preserved it as a kind of makeshift shrine, ready for Audrey if she ever came home.

But it was an amalgam of both. The white daybed I always envied remained intact yet a new dresser and a bureau replaced the bookshelf and vanity. A couple posters—shirtless centerfolds from trashy teen magazines—drooped from the walls, and even after more than a decade, the creases had never relaxed. But on the back of the door, yellowed tape was all that remained in the wake of forsaken décor. I tried to remember what poster Audrey had placed there, but my memory drifted away from me like deadwood in a black sea.

I listened for my lost friend, and the house remembered for me. There in her sanctuary, the echo of Audrey's candied voice fused with the eggshell white paint. The room cradled her murmurs from bygone sleepovers when she had leaned close to me, that warm breath whispering into my ear about Daniel.

"I love him, Kaylee. I really do. I'm going to marry him someday."

My question was always the same. "Can I be a bridesmaid?"

"Of course, you can, silly. You can be the maid of honor."

"But I don't want to be a maid."

Together, we'd giggle until someone hushed us. Then we'd laugh a little bit more.

Mrs. Anderson nudged into the room and stood near me. "I thought you'd be in here."

I fixated on the empty daybed. "Did she leave a note?"

"My dear girl, jilted women always leave notes."

"Did she mention me?"

"She did."

"May I read it?"

"No, you may not." She stepped back and inspected me. "I need you to leave now."

Back at the welcome mat, I turned to Mrs. Anderson, my eyes wide and arms shaking. "She wants my baby."

She shrugged, one arm resting against the doorframe. "It should be her child with Daniel, not yours."

"Please," I said. "If you could forgive me, maybe Audrey can too."

"But I have no interest in exonerating you, Kaylee. If I had my way, you'd die of guilt." This time, she did slam the door, abandoning me in the bare sunlight with nothing more than my memories of Audrey to accompany me home.

Around nine, Daniel phoned to say goodnight. He talked about his day and how stressful conventions were and a list of business complaints that I neither understood nor cared to hear.

Fatigued with talk of spreadsheets, I interrupted. "Do you ever think about Audrey?" It was the first time since she died we'd spoken her name between us.

He hesitated. "What made you remember her?"

"I never forgot."

"Kaylee," Daniel said, and in my mind, I could see him tilt his head and flash me that half-smile I loved. "She did what she did. That's not our fault. We fell in love, and I won't apologize for that."

I nodded and hoped he could envision my response the same way I imagined his.

We said I love you, and I bid him farewell. It was time to prepare for Audrey.

An old turntable sat in the corner of our bedroom. I ran my hand across the lid and blew the film of dust from my skin. My fingers fumbled with the needle and managed to drop it at the outside edge of the record.

As I rested on the bed, the light still on, I worried the couch might be a better place to wait. Audrey might not expect that. She might head into the bedroom out of habit. But if she started her evening treks in the living room, I would just meet her sooner on the couch.

The melody of the flamenco guitar merged with the scratching along the hardwood. I sang, loud and out of tune, to drown the sound of both.

Don't look at the doorway, I thought. *Don't watch for her. She's not there. Pretend she's not there.*

But the record ended, and the scratches continued. And on this evening, she crooned lyrics as well.

"Kaylee. Kaylee."

The crystalline voice approached with sing-song elegance. The turntable rotated, and the speakers emitted a blank din. I wanted to yank the cord from the wall and obliterate the noise, but Audrey appeared, face to the floor, and called my name again.

"Kaylee."

I stared at her, but she moved toward me anyway. Perhaps I never stopped her at all. Perhaps it was always Daniel that kept her at bay, though he never knew she was there.

Her gnarled fingers gripped the fringe of the rug, and she breached the imaginary border I worked for years to defend.

"Audrey, please," I said. "Please don't."

I moved across the mattress to Daniel's side. Audrey shifted around the front of the bed to reach me. Her hands clawed at the comforter and I eyed the door, wondering if I could make it down the hall before she could seize me. But she would return. She'd never stop. I'd earned this.

Wrenching herself onto the bed, Audrey sat next to me. She smelled of faint floral, and her skin remained as perfect as it was in the senior picture her mother cast out. My bare feet dug into the sheet as I pushed against the headboard to escape her. With a graceful surge of her body, she leaned toward me, and I realized where the cinnamon and roses of her parents' house had gone.

There was no decay on her. No sign of what she'd done to herself. No inkling of age. Just a beautiful young woman perched near her friend.

She pressed her lips to my ear, her soft breath warming my skin.

"Kaylee, I want to tell you something."

Like her face, the voice remained unchanged, and on hearing it again, I suddenly remembered the missing poster in her room. It was an impressionist painting of Victorian ladies in a garden. My gift for her twenty-second birthday. Her last birthday.

Tears salting my cheeks, I wished I had listened in Sunday school and could recite a prayer, any prayer. Audrey would remember one.

The saccharine rhythm stirred the air. "I only wanted to tell you what I've done."

"What, Audrey?" I closed my eyes as her red curls fell against my face. "What have you done?"

"You'll see soon. Just know it's for you, Kaylee. It's for you."

I didn't move for hours. I feared if I opened my eyes, I would find her still sitting there.

Outside, the cars whirred up and down the suburban street, and the newspaper ricocheted off the front door. The moment the heat of daylight streamed through the window, I phoned 911, and an ambulance took me to the county hospital.

"Run every test you can." I shed my clothes and climbed into the white gown. "There's something wrong with my baby."

Three hours and a litany of needles and tubes later, an ER nurse comforted me with a stiff, patronizing smile.

"Darling, there's nothing wrong," she said. "You have one healthy pregnancy."

I nodded, the charts and sonograms mocking me from their roost on the wall.

"Do you need a ride home?"

"I can walk," I said.

As I crossed the parking lot, I called Daniel. An unfamiliar voice answered.

"Are you Daniel Cooke's wife?"

"Yes," I said. "Who is this?"

Brain aneurysm is the nicer term for a stroke. Nobody thinks a hearty man of thirty can die of a disease associated with the elderly, so doctors say brain aneurysm to help the family make sense of it. But I knew what killed Daniel, and it wasn't a tiny blood vessel giving way.

"Who found him?" I crouched on the pavement and prodded a piece of gravel along a crack in the sidewalk.

"A coworker," the voice said.

"How'd a coworker get into his room?"

From the other end of the line, there was nothing but white noise.

"Did the coworker happen to be female?" I tucked my index finger against my thumb for leverage and flicked the piece of gravel into the air.

"Yes."

"Please keep the details to yourself," I said, "but send my husband's body home. I'd like to bury him this week."

I stayed with my parents while they made the preparations for Daniel. The next three days, all I could do was lie in my old bed and sob. Audrey never came to visit, and I imagined her in my house, resting on my side of the mattress. She could wait for as long as she needed to finish me too.

Roses were the blossom of choice for the calling hours, and as I stood in my mourning garb next to the coffin, I gagged at the scent.

"Can you send the flowers away?" I covered my mouth. "They're making me sick."

My mother vanquished the reminders of Audrey, and I thanked her.

Faces poured into the cramped room. Like an assembly line, the stream of bereaved kissed my cheeks and offered psalms of sympathy. I pretended I was someone else.

A hand suddenly gripped mine, gripped with a fragile yet unearthly grace.

"I'm sorry about your loss, Kaylee," Mrs. Anderson said. "Truly, I am."

I hadn't seen her enter through the foyer, and I wondered if she could materialize like her spectral daughter. I studied the features so like Audrey's. She embraced me, and my body collapsed into her arms. We remained together in the center of the room for a long time, not caring that we blocked others from the casket.

Before she departed, Mrs. Anderson shuffled a small envelope into my hands. "I brought you a copy of Audrey's note," she said. "I don't know if it will help now or make things worse, but I think she would want you to read it."

I pulled myself from the crowd and retired to an empty hallway near a vacant viewing room. The glue on the fresh envelope released its hold, and my fingers gripped the letter that had terrified me since my mother took me aside during my wedding reception and told me Audrey was gone.

Clean black letters with buoyant curves covered the page, and I recognized the handwriting from the surreptitious notes we passed during study halls and recesses. My eyes closed as I amassed the nerve to read it. Then I inhaled and began.

Dearest Daniel,

You robbed me of my happiness. You robbed me of my life. You even robbed me of my best friend. I don't know what the next life holds, but in this moment before I'm about to meet the one who made me, I swear with all the life left in me that I won't let you hurt her like you hurt me.

Yours, Now & Forever,
Audrey

※

For the first time, I felt the baby kick. My hand fluttered to my stomach on instinct, and I lingered in the hallway of the funeral parlor and didn't move or speak for almost an hour. Guests waltzed past, their arms and shoulders and hair brushing against me as they offered condolences. But not until the overhead lights dimmed and my parents grasped my hands did I stir from my position. They asked if I wanted to stay with them for a while longer. I requested to go home.

I sat awake every night for a week. Audrey never returned.

THE FIVE-DAY SUMMER CAMP

*O*H, *WHAT FUN you'll have!*

That was all we heard from our parents the morning we left for camp.

My older sister Madeline rolled her eyes. "They pretend I haven't already been there."

We had nothing to pack—the camp would issue our uniforms when we arrived—so I sat cross-legged on the floor of our room as Madeline made her bed. She was careful about it, tucking this corner and smoothing that wrinkle, as though this was the most important task she'd ever performed. Our mother called upstairs to tell us to hurry so we wouldn't miss the bus, but I didn't move, not until Madeline was finished.

Nearby, the comforter on my mattress was undisturbed. I never slept where I belonged. Every night, once the lights went out—all over the city at nine o'clock on the dot—I would creep across the floor and curl up beside my sister. She was warm, and her skin smelled sweet like cinnamon, like a home we'd never known. Tucked beneath her blanket, I invented silly stories of us floating on clouds or swimming a mile beneath the ocean, tales that usually made her smile. But last night, she'd shaken her head and said, "I won't always be here, Arabella. You need to grow up and stop hiding in make-believe."

I pretended not to hear her. She was always morose right before camp, and this year was worse than most. This was her third year. Her last chance.

"And what if the rumors are true?" our mother was asking when Madeline and I came downstairs. "What if it runs in families?"

"Everything will be fine," our father said, his tenor steady as the tides. "The men at camp know best."

When they noticed us standing there, they smiled as if everything was perfectly normal. This was how they always looked. Our parents never screamed or cried or even frowned, except on Red Days, and this wasn't a Red Day. This was a normal morning, and they were a normal mother and father.

"We hope to see you soon," they said to Madeline before turning to me and adjusting my shoulders so I wouldn't slouch. "Did you make your bed?"

I smiled. "Of course."

"You're a liar," Madeline said when we were alone on the sidewalk. "You haven't made that bed in years."

"Nope." I looped my arm in hers. "And I never will."

She laughed, and the crisp melody of her joy was like a most beautiful rapture.

"What a dreadful little sister I have," she said, and hugged me so close I could barely breathe. Above us, a small red light pulsed at the top of the streetlamp. We pretended not to see it. We weren't supposed to know about the neighborhood cameras. There were many things we shouldn't know, but knew anyhow. Adults always thought kids were too stupid to figure out the truth, and sometimes, it was easier to let them go on believing that.

Up and down the sidewalk, other kids like us waited for the bus, and all the parents grinned from their front porches and bid us farewell. In five days, they would drive to camp and retrieve us—or retrieve *most* of us—but the yellow bus took us there. That was the rule.

For the bonding experience, said the official itinerary I'd memorized when it arrived in the mail last month. *Your children must feel like they belong.*

My heart fluttering in my throat, I waved once to our parents. Madeline never looked back to say goodbye.

※※

Day One Itinerary
Arrival at Camp
Student Orientation
Snack
Lights Out

※※

The bus was crowded and hot and smelled as salty as fresh tears. Everyone tittered in their seats, flinging insults and spitballs. Most of the kids were fifteen like me, first years who'd never been to camp. Madeline was the only third year among us.

"Freak," someone yelled at her, and the strident voices laughed in refrain.

She and I huddled together in the back. "Don't worry," she whispered. "I'll protect you."

It was dusk when the camp came into view against a scrim of velvet mountains and skeletal trees. Years ago, kids spent June through August here, but now it was a revolving door of classes all summer. We filed off the bus past the last students, who were graduating in their bleached white tunics. They smiled and waved at us with an odd little salute. I waved back, but Madeline grasped my hand and pulled me away from them, marching us along the walkway and past a stout cabin. Next to it was a strange metal contraption the size of a work shed. Through a thin chimney, it spewed ash and smoke into the air.

"What's that?" I asked, but Madeline said nothing.

At the entrance of the main lodge, a row of men arrayed in peacoats greeted us with stern faces. The air shimmered with July humidity, but even swathed in layers of wool, these figures never thawed.

"Welcome," they said, but I didn't believe them.

Inside, the lodge radiated pine cleaner and something vaguely rotten, like a mouse caught in last week's trap. Posters covered every wall. One announcement listed the camp's rules, and another said in black block letters, IF YOU SEE SOMETHING, SAY SOMETHING. My favorite featured a cartoon face with an animated expression and a slogan beneath it. YOU SHOULD SMILE ALL THE TIME.

I grinned back at the poster, eager to oblige.

The lodge was Spartan and consisted of a large mess hall with long wooden benches for eating and listening to lectures, a narrow den filled with taxidermy animals, and our sleeping quarters, where rows of metal beds were lined up like graves.

The men in peacoats locked the doors behind the last student and handed us each a white tunic.

"Banish the old," they said, and demanded we change right there in front of one another.

We were all red-faced at the idea, but we knew not to argue with government men, so Madeline sheltered me as I stripped down and yanked the muslin over my head.

After we were dressed and our old clothes discarded, the men ordered us to the wooden benches for orientation.

114

"Pay attention," they said, and clicked off the lights. "There will be a test at the end."

A gentleman with a serious face materialized on the screen alongside a little girl who smiled as though she'd never had a bad thought in her life.

"The best people are happy people," the man said. "And at the end of your stay here, that's exactly what you'll be. A good child. A happy child."

The little girl chortled. "And who wouldn't want that?"

I scratched at the collar of my tunic. No wonder Madeline was glum. Three years of bad lectures and bad fashions would make anyone grumpy.

"These five days are the beginning of your new life," the man in the video said, his face comically hangdog for someone lecturing on happiness. "A life free of pain, misery, and deceit."

"Hear that, Arabella?" Madeline asked without inflection. "You'll lose your favorite hobby. No more lying. No more make-believe."

Her eyes glistened in the glow of the screen like she was ready to cry.

"It's okay," I said, and squeezed her hand. "I'll find a new hobby."

When the video was over, the men in peacoats distributed white wafer bars, and sent us to bed. In our shared room, the other kids gobbled down their snacks with gusto, but Madeline shook her head, and when no one was looking, she tucked both our wafers under her mattress.

"But I'm hungry," I whined.

"Not safe," she said.

I snuffed and leaned against the window. Outside, the metal chimney near the cabin no longer seeped ash. It was peaceful now.

At nine o'clock, the lights went out, and the others soon quieted. When the last voice faded to a murmur, I tossed off my sheets and crawled to Madeline.

"Back to your own bed," she whispered. "Before someone sees."

But I didn't want to leave, so I coiled tighter around her and made little snoring noises as though I was already asleep.

"Faker," she said, and pinched my arm until I giggled.

"Where should we go tonight?" I rested my head in the crook of her arm. "How about the moon, where we can dine on craters of cheese? Or maybe Mars. We've never been to Mars."

Madeline sighed. "We've never been anywhere, Arabella. Except our own neighborhood."

"And here," I said. "We've been here too."

But this place wasn't so different from home. On the ceiling, a camera winked at us in the darkness, its red light smoldering and strange like a distant, unknowable planet.

※

Day Two Itinerary
Breakfast
All-Day Lecture
Communal Supper
Lights Out

※

At breakfast, Madeline stared at the floor and ate nothing.

"The food is poison," she said. "To make us more docile. Like livestock to the slaughter."

I didn't know if that was true, but I was too starved to care, so I devoured a heaping bowl of porridge. The mush was bland yet metallic.

Before the day's lecture, the men in peacoats taught us

a new kind of wave, the same one the graduating class used yesterday.

"It shows respect," they said, which made sense, since I'd seen our parents do it whenever government men zoomed past on their daily patrols.

I perfected the movement, up and out with the arm, but Madeline's hands rested in her lap.

"You'll be sorry," the men said.

The lights faded, and the little girl and serious-faced man were back with a diagram of a medical syringe.

"Shots are never pleasant," the little girl said, and scrunched up her nose. "But it's a small tradeoff for happiness, don't you think?"

"And the good news," the man said, "is once you're treated successfully, you're inoculated for life."

"That means no more shots." The little girl grinned. "Super cool, right?"

I scoffed. So far, nothing here was cool or fun.

Dinner that night was more porridge, bland as breakfast, and I choked down only half my rations. Madeline had nothing at all.

"Aren't you hungry?" I asked, but she just shrugged.

The other kids were already asleep when the lights went out at nine. I was tired too, but I couldn't rest, not without Madeline. I climbed up on her mattress, and pretended not to notice the tears streaking her cheeks.

She gathered me in her arms. "Where are we tonight in your universe?"

"Saturn," I said. "Waltzing together on the rings."

"You can't waltz on Saturn's rings, Arabella." She sniffled. "They're made of sand. You'd fall through."

"I can waltz on them if I want," I said.

"I wish I could do something," she murmured, and I knew she wasn't thinking of Saturn anymore. "I wish I could get you away from here."

I buried my face in her lavender-scented hair. This wasn't the only time she'd talked like this.

"Let's run away," she'd said when she returned the first year from camp.

"And where would we go?" I'd asked, wide-eyed.

"Anywhere far from here."

But there was nowhere for us except my imaginary journeys, and those made her smile so seldom now. I feared she might never smile again.

"Don't worry." I squeezed her hand as the camera light burned a halo into my eyes. "We'll be okay."

Madeline swallowed a sob and turned her back to me, so that her body was silhouetted against the window, against the outline of the solemn chimney. Maybe she wanted to be alone, but I didn't care. I nuzzled against the stiff fabric of her tunic and slipped into a dreamless sleep.

❧❧

Day Three Itinerary
Breakfast
Morning Lecture
Afternoon Rest
Lights Out

❧❧

In the next video, the serious-faced man and the little girl recited a lot of technical words and talked about flooding brains with things called neurotransmitters.

I tried to listen, but the half bowl of porridge from breakfast sloshed in my belly and doubled me over the bench.

"You okay?" Madeline asked, her worried eyes the color of

118

sand dollars.

"I'm fine," I wheezed.

On the screen, the little girl smiled like she knew a secret. "We've already told you how happy people are the most productive," she said. "But even with the best treatments, there are sometimes momentary lapses."

"This is known as spontaneous recovery," the man said. "And it's why we have Red Days. As a healthy outlet for unhealthy emotion."

I rasped out a laugh. As if Red Days were so healthy. Last year, our neighbor Mr. Georges lost his plate glass window when our father tossed him through it. And that wasn't the first mishap. Since I was in kindergarten, we'd lost three houses on our street to Red Day fires. Accidents, the government called them.

"Most of you are good children," the man in the video continued. "And good children will leave here smiling. But if your first visit doesn't take, that's okay. We'll try again next year. And if you return for a third visit, we have a special treatment just for you."

Madeline flinched next to me. I wanted to hold her hand and comfort her, but my fingers had gone numb. My entire body was numb.

"And if all three treatments don't work," the little girl said with a wide, toothy grin, "then we have a very special home for these very special people."

"Liars!" Madeline shot to her feet. "You're all liars!"

In the gloom, the shapes from the video flickered on her face like shadow puppets.

"Enjoy your treatment," the man said. "And we'll see you soon."

The whole room went black, but even in the dark, my sister glowed with conviction. The men in peacoats closed in around her, but she flailed and spit and screamed.

I wanted to scream with her, but I couldn't move. I could only watch, as one by one, the other kids slumped on the benches like dominoes in a line. I inhaled a ragged breath, and the world dissolved in a glimmering gray.

The last thing I heard was my sister calling my name.

⁂

<u>Day Four Itinerary</u>
Morning Exams
Afternoon Interviews
Lights Out

⁂

At dawn, I woke in my own bed and didn't remember getting there. The others were in their beds as well, and on the undersides of all our left arms, we wore matching bruises—tiny marks, wide enough for a needle. A tattoo of our five days at camp.

Only my sister's mattress was empty, the sheets clean and unruffled.

There was no breakfast for us. Our stomachs were too sick for food.

"This is normal," the men in peacoats said when a blond girl with a wilted ponytail retched up yellow bile on the floor of the mess hall. "You'll soon feel better."

We nodded and mumbled and sagged on the benches, as the lights dimmed for Day 4's video. This one was different—there was no pair of familiar narrators. Instead, there were images. Thousands of them. Pictures of torn flesh and mortar explosions and mushroom-shaped finales. Sprays of red as bright and beautiful as the topography of Mars, and bodies split open like cracked walnuts.

120

This was the test the men promised. Along the far wall, they observed us, taking notes if someone screamed or cried or broke in some way that showed the treatment wasn't successful. And some of us did. Several kids my age begged for their parents, begged to know why, begged to be anywhere but in this room.

"That's okay," the men said, and escorted the sobbing children back to their beds. "You'll always have next year."

With my hands folded on my lap, I didn't weep or shriek. I didn't feel anything at all.

After the video ended, the men summoned us one at a time into the den. The other kids marched past me, in and out of the room. They all looked alike now, their posture erect, their faces blazing with an uncanny rosiness. They smiled as if the sentiment had always lived like a parasite inside their chests. This is what we were promised. We were happy, and would be happy forever.

When at last the men called my name, I stood with shoulders back and chin tipped up to face the world. My days of slouching were over. Our parents would be proud.

In the room with graying deer heads looming on the walls, the men in peacoats waited for me.

"Hello, Arabella."

"Hello," I said in a clear, bright timbre. This was the first time I had spoken today, and in a way, it was the first time I had ever spoken, at least with my real voice.

The men took my blood pressure and jotted down my pulse and they asked me dozens of questions, but I was a good child, and did well every time.

"We were concerned you might be like your sister," they said.

I smiled. "She and I aren't the same."

"Congratulations," they said, and stamped my file.

My lips parted to ask them where Madeline was, what

they had done to her last night. But that wouldn't be appropriate. Good children answered questions. We never asked them.

With the sun setting on the camp, I retreated alone to my bed. All around me, the failed students curled like aborted infants, and over their mournful cries, I strained to hear my sister's voice. But this time, no one was calling to me.

⚜

Day Five Itinerary
Celebratory Breakfast
Exit Lecture
Graduation

⚜

Our final breakfast was a fine meal. Stacked pancakes and boats of syrup and little pats of yellow butter, none of it bland or metallic. We gulped freshly squeezed orange juice and prattled to one another and grinned until our faces ached. This meal was special, because this was our graduation day, the first day of our new lives.

Afterwards, I returned once more to the sleeping quarters. The blanket on my bed was tangled, and my sister's was not. The world was inverted, just the way the men liked it.

Through the window, the lone cabin was a silent phantom against the horizon. The nearby chimney was not yet smoldering, and no ash lilted like charred rose petals in the air. There was still time for one last request.

The men in peacoats assembled like tin soldiers in the mess hall, and I saluted them.

"Yes?" they asked.

"I would like to see my sister."

"Why?" Their dark voices thrummed like air bubbles in

122

my blood.

I smiled. "To say goodbye, of course."

At once, their faces softened. This was the reply of a good child, and you couldn't deny a good child, especially on her graduation day.

One of the men escorted me the hundred steps to the cabin, his hand on my spine to push me along. On our way, we passed the metal behemoth with the skinny chimney. Up close, it looked smaller. More person-sized. Madeline-sized.

The man unlocked the door. Inside, the walls were sterile white, and the room stank of bleach and urine.

"Be quick," he said to me, and we stepped through the doorway.

My sister was crumpled in the corner, her hair glued to her cheeks with sweat, and needle marks along her arms in a constellation of deep blue bruises.

There was no special treatment. Just the same treatment, the same shot ten times over.

I knelt to the cold tile, and the infinite weight of my sister's body drooped against me.

Her eyes webbed with red, she gazed at me, and a warm shock of electricity shot through my body. She was stronger than they ever realized. What they did to her should have left a void where my sister was, but not one iota of her had changed. The men exhausted their options, and here she was, my Madeline.

"I love you, Arabella," she said, her voice hoarse and hushed and meant only for me. "I'm so sorry."

"Don't worry," I whispered. "I'll protect you."

I reached for her hand, but the man grabbed my arm and wrenched me to my feet. The searing pain surprised me. After all, you were only permitted to manhandle a woman on Red Days. But wearing a peacoat must have exempted him from the usual rules.

"What did she say to you?" he demanded.

"That it worked," I said, smiling. "She told me the procedure worked."

There was a long, agonizing moment when the whole world threatened to shatter.

The man looked from me to my sister and back again. He inspected me from top to bottom. My posture was correct. My voice, clear and bright and obedient, was correct. Everything about me was perfectly correct. I couldn't be lying, because good children didn't lie. And didn't yesterday's tests confirm I was a good child?

From the floor, Madeline peered up at me, not understanding at first. I was almost afraid she wouldn't understand at all, that she might ruin it for us both.

With a gentle hand, I guided her up to meet me. "Reexamine her if you don't believe me."

Madeline was too weak to walk on her own, so I joined her in the den for the tests. The heinous images flashed again and again, and the men grilled her with questions, but with me at her side, she was flawless. I wrapped my fingers around hers and squeezed her hand every time she shouldn't flinch, and I stroked her wrist to calm her as they measured blood pressure and heart rate.

I was always good at make-believe. Now Madeline was good at make-believe too.

"Congratulations," the men said, their eyes black as cancer, as they stamped her file.

In the mess hall with the other kids, we watched one last video.

"Thank you for joining us," the serious-faced man said.

The little girl saluted goodbye. "We wish you the best with your wonderful new life!"

Parents swarmed the camp like ants around road kill, and with no ash in the air, graduation was a joyous occasion. Our own mother and father beamed while Madeline and I collected our diplomas and posed for a hundred pictures in our white tunics.

The new students arrived on bright yellow school buses, and I smiled at them and saluted and memorized their faces, trying to pick out the ones like us, the good children who were skilled at make-believe. Someday, Madeline and I might find them again. We might meet them in a smoke-filled room where we'd need a special password just to get through the door. We might reminisce and laugh at these men in their peacoats, by then gray and faded and past their prime, and we might laugh at this camp and laugh at what we'll be planning, what we'll do when we're older and stronger and ready.

And in the meantime, if a chattering neighbor thought they saw something and should say something, that would be okay too. Madeline and I would simply wait for a Red Day. Because everybody knew accidents sometimes happened on Red Days.

Together, we climbed into the backseat of our parents' car, and soon, the camp vanished in the rearview mirror. With my sister beside me, I smiled my widest smile and squeezed her hand until my veins ached. Our parents were right.

Oh, what fun we'll have!

SKIN
LIKE HONEY
AND LACE

I'M MAKING ESPRESSO for a man in an ill-fitting business suit when Emily shimmies up to the cash register, arrayed in a body made of other people's skins.

"Hello, Clare," she says and smiles.

The frothing pitcher steams in my hand, and I pretend to look surprised to see her. We both know I'm not. Even before the front door swung open, and the rush of the street seeped into the coffeehouse—the backfires of clunker cars and cat-calls from the drug dealers on the sidewalk—I could feel her coming. My skin prickles whenever she's near.

I say nothing as she drums her fingers on the counter and inspects the list of overpriced drinks affixed to the wall. Her face, molded with layer atop layer of new flesh, is different every time we meet. But I always recognize her. The curves of her bones peek through. The same silken bones beneath my flesh.

"Figured it was you when I turned the corner," she says.

"Your skin sings differently than the others. Like famine and lullabies."

And your skin sings like a dog in heat, I want to say.

I gnaw my bottom lip. "How's Genevieve?"

"Better than you," Emily says. "You look terrible."

She laughs, her subtle way of reminding me there are people here in this coffeehouse, just waiting to be peeled like hardboiled eggs.

Why not steal a piece, Clare? that cut-glass voice of hers murmurs through our skins. *You know you're overdue.*

I scratch a flaky patch on my arm. "I get by."

Emily leans closer. "Why don't I take you out tonight?" Her eyes flash, and the pity she feels for me thrums through my body. "The girls and I are meeting in the Strip at seven."

I slide the mug of espresso down to the end of the bar and turn back to her. "Sure, I guess."

I play it off as if I don't care, as if I haven't spent the last ten months inventing one-sided conversations with Emily, pretending I could convince her to stay.

"Perfect," she says. "See you then."

She leaves without ordering, her long ponytail swinging like a whip behind her.

After she's gone, I glance at my hand that held the frothing pitcher. The skin is red and angry. While Emily was here, I burned myself. I never felt a thing.

I don't remember my first layer of skin. I don't remember meeting Emily either. These came before. Too long ago to matter.

What I do remember: I didn't want this body.

My bones were beautiful. Exquisite and bare, the color of pewter, encasing me like a shell. Back then, I required no skin. None of us did, not Emily or the few others like us. This husk is only for blending in.

"Makes life easier if nobody knows about the bones," Emily used to say.

But nothing about this is easy.

⁂

I meet Emily at the last bar in the Strip District. The rest of the businesses here—the trendy restaurants and the dress boutiques and the dive clubs—closed down years ago. The whole city is practically closed down. For decades, this place was something straight out of P.T. Barnum's wet dream. A year-round circus and sideshow and a cut-rate amusement park with bumper cars and shell games and a carousel. Now the once-bustling boardwalk along the pier is abandoned. Nothing left there except empty buildings and one sleazy watering hole that could outlast cockroaches.

Emily's at a high-top table in the corner with a gaggle of girls. I recognize them—we share some of the same skin—but I don't remember their names. They probably don't remember mine either. We're no better than strangers.

When she sees me, Emily gives me that sweetheart smile. "Glad you could make it, darling."

I reach out for her hand, but she drifts away from me as Genevieve arrives at the table, carrying a round of drinks for everyone but me.

I tuck myself into the corner, and dig at the dry patch on my arm.

Techno music blares over the speakers, and the dance floor overflows with young men and women, communing like red ants, their sweat heavy on the air. The girls and I stand back and inspect their skins. We only need one for the night, but even one is hard to find. Especially for me.

When drunk boys with glistening flesh thrust their nicotine-smudged hands at my body and offer me free drinks, I always draw up my nose and shake my head, and they call me "bitch" or "tease" before they stomp off.

That's why my flesh is slowly rotting off my bones. Because I won't say yes.

I should be better at this. When we were young, Emily taught me how to hunt. Who taught her, I'll never know, but she gave me what I need to survive. A flask of sun-yellow oil, and a sheathed knife. It doesn't take much to get what we want.

After her third drink, Emily makes our choice—a guy in a ratty sports jersey with a logo of a hockey stick and a penguin emblazoned on the back. We have no team like that around here. He's a tourist, and he's alone. A perfect mark.

She whispers to him, and he leads her down the block to his seedy beachfront motel. The girls and I follow a few steps behind, and wait outside the room.

"Come on in," Emily calls to us after a moment.

Inside, it stinks of the oil, nauseating as turpentine. On the bed, the boy's undressed and dozing, his chest a sallow, jaundiced color. Emily probably told him the oil was foreplay. In a way, it is. A couple drops on the skin is all it takes to put him into a dream.

"You do the cutting, Clare," Emily says as she slips out of her silk dress. "You've always been the best at that part."

I shed my clothes and kneel before the bed.

The first incision is the most important. Choose right, and there will be no blood, no chance this boy in the garish sports jersey will know what we've done to him. Tomorrow, he'll awaken with what looks like a mild sunburn. No surprise really. He spent the day in a beach town, after all.

Choose wrong, and the blood will come. And it might not stop, not until we have a mess to clean up.

I wriggle the tip of my knife into his lower abdomen and trim off a thin cut of flesh as pale and translucent as Queen Anne's lace. There's no pigment in this layer. Pigment comes deeper in the skin. We don't go that far. We try not to be covetous, try not to take more than we need.

Over and over, I slice his chest and pass the pieces down the line, as though I'm carving a Christmas ham. The girls and I paste ourselves together like paper dolls, covering our rough patches first. The oil works on us too, gluing the new skin to our hides.

The flesh takes hours to blend with ours, so we gather on the floor to wait. We need to give it time. We can't live without the skin.

"It fuses to our bones," Emily told me once. "It's part of us. If the skin dies, so do we."

As we sit cross-legged, Emily places her hand on my bare thigh. Genevieve watches us, but says nothing.

The boy murmurs through heavy dreams, his body pink and raw but alive. At last, his flesh merges on the strata of our skins.

Bodies buzzing, the girls and I lock the door behind us and scatter into the night.

On the street, Emily hooks her arm in mine. "Walk with me for a while."

I squint at her. "Won't Genevieve be jealous?"

"Maybe." Emily grins. "But she'll get over it."

We stroll together through downtown. Half the buildings are boarded up, faded FOR LEASE signs stamped on windows. At the end of Main Street, the concrete turns to sand, and we stand on the border of the old boardwalk. A rusted chain link fence with a NO TRESPASSING warning holds us back.

I sigh, and the sentiment ripples through our skins. In a tragic way, we belong here. This tourist town dies a little each day, and with our bodies always wilting, so do we.

Emily tugs my arm. "Don't get melancholy, darling."

She kisses me hard on the mouth, on lips that aren't mine. Not one exposed piece of this body belongs to me. She's kissing a stranger.

I hold tight to her hand, but she pulls away from me.

"See you around, Clare."

※

And just like that, Emily vanishes from my life. Not completely, though. Our skin bridges us together. She vibrates through my body until everything else is white noise. Her joy tastes like cotton candy melting in my mouth. Her disappointment is like copper, like blood rising up the back of my throat.

Behind the counter at the coffeehouse, my eyes glaze as the soccer moms and moody hipsters bark their orders at me. Cortado. Americano. Macchiato. The flesh on my arms withers, but I take no new skin. Why would I want these people on my body when simply frothing their lattes every morning disgusts me?

It's early spring, a chill lingering in the brackish air, when Emily meets someone. From across town, I feel his flesh fuse with hers. A "regular," she soon calls him, and tosses Genevieve from her bed. Emily loves this new boy, or at least she loves what he does to her.

All night, I roam the streets, the taste of salty tears on my tongue. At the edge of town, the ocean mumbles louder than Emily. I can escape her here, if for a moment. I peel back a weak section of the boardwalk fence and crawl inside.

The old thoroughfare is hushed and crumbling. Faded murals promising an authentic Fiji mermaid decorate every wall. In a fever dream, I stumble past the graveyard of abandoned rides and derelict food carts with splintered planking nailed over the windows. Next to the rusted skeleton of the

Tilt-O-Whirl, a figure slips out of the shadows.

A woman with skin like fresh cream.

I blink at her, half-convinced she's an illusion.

"What do you want?" she asks, scowling.

Her flesh gleams in the moonlight, and my mouth waters just looking at it.

"A cup of tea would be nice," I say.

Her name is Nathalie. She lives here in a loft among the ghosts of bygone summers.

"This apartment used to house traveling vaudeville acts," she says, and shows me inside. Her voice is bright, as though she's been waiting years to tell someone this story.

The whole boardwalk belonged to her family, but after a legacy of empty bank accounts and emptier bottles, she's the only one left. Now boxes of freeze-dried food and faded carnival memorabilia pile up in every corner. She's exiled from the world, the heir of forgotten magic.

"I'm alone too," I say.

At her kitchen table, we sit together and sip chamomile from steaming mugs. The heat likely burns my lips, but I can't feel anything except the weight of wanting her.

She sniffs the air, her nose curled. "What's your perfume?"

I pick at my flaking shoulder. "I'm not wearing perfume."

It's the oil she smells on me. I smell it too, caustic and soaked deep into my skin. I could take a thousand showers and never fully wash it away.

I fumble through a stack of mail-order catalogs on the table. "So you don't go out much?"

"Why would I?" The question, defiant and cold, sounds like a challenge. "What's out there worth seeing?"

"Nothing," I say, and mean it.

We finish our tea in silence. I thank her and move for the door. Her face goes gray as if she expected me to stay. She's lonely, same as me. She doesn't know yet what I'll do to her.

I should be better than this. She was kind to me, and I should leave her alone, but that skin. I need that beautiful skin.

At the door, I turn back. "May I see you again?"

She hesitates. "If you want," she says.

I smile.

᎒᎒᎒

Every night for a week, I venture to the boardwalk, and like a serf before a princess, I bring Nathalie gifts. A bag of Gala apples. A head of iceberg lettuce. Silly little offerings that make her smile. These are the closest she's been to real food since the day the last concession stand was boarded up. In her loft, she dances in the kitchen, dicing up the produce, and singing off-key to an old cassette of Tom Petty's *Wildflowers*.

"It's my anthem," she says, and blushes when she sees me watching.

I haven't touched her yet, not even a handshake. I'm waiting for the ideal moment, but exactly when that moment will come, I don't know.

I'm halfway back to the boardwalk when my skin burns as though I'm being flayed alive. The girls need me. My real, grotesque life needs me.

At the same beachfront motel, they titter in a second-floor room, panicked as headless hens in a coop. A lifeless man reclines on the yellowed mattress, and Genevieve quivers nearby, her hands stained red.

"It was an accident," she murmurs.

Emily coos and runs her fingers through a tangle in Genevieve's hair. "Don't worry, darling," she says. "It happens to everyone."

Not true. It's never happened to me. It's never happened to Emily either.

The girls and I strip the soiled sheets from the bed and

bleach the bloodied box springs.

"Could you do the next part, Clare?" Emily smiles as if slicing up dead bodies like tomatoes is the most normal request.

The man's eyes are open. I flip him on his belly, so I won't have to see those dilated pupils, vacant as tide pools, staring at me. His flesh is still warm. That's good. Heat makes it easier to divide the body.

The girls and I absorb all the skin, even the fat, and we devour the heart and the other organs too. My stomach cramps, and I gag up mouthfuls of bile. We all gag. This isn't ideal. There's too much flesh on us—and in us. But this is the rule. The cleanest way to hide a body is to ensure no body is left to find.

Emily grinds up the bones into flour and promises to bake Genevieve soul cakes for breakfast.

"I won't go with you," Genevieve says, sobbing. "Not back to that horrible boy in your bed."

"We'll talk about it later," Emily says as we gather on the floor to sleep. This much skin will take until tomorrow to settle on us.

I curl in the corner, and a small, misshapen pomegranate topples out of my jacket pocket. This was meant for Nathalie. I bite into the bitter flesh, and the blood of the fruit spills across my lips.

Emily nestles next to me, and we fall asleep, her hand draped across my heart.

※

An hour before dawn, something rips inside of us, and we awaken, sweat-caked and moaning like a deranged choir. But there's no blood. No withering. It isn't our pain we're feeling.

Genevieve's gone. At first light, we hear the report on the

local radio station. The Coast Guard discovered what was left of her on the shore, the gristle the ocean tossed back. A membrane of skin, but no bone.

"They won't find the rest of her," Emily says. "She's settled to the bottom by now."

I choke back rueful tears.

Still queasy, we flee the motel, and I walk alone in the amber morning.

At the boardwalk, Nathalie's asleep in bed. I watch her dreaming, my body bloated beneath too many pieces of patchwork skin. Another layer might be too much, but I don't care. I need something on me that's mine. Something I want.

I climb quietly onto the mattress, gripping the knife and oil. But before I lift the blade, Nathalie opens her eyes.

Her jaw clenches. "Will you kill me?"

"No," I say. "If I'm careful, you won't feel a thing."

Her chest rises and falls like a restless sea. "Why?"

"It's how I survive."

A ridiculous answer. She deserves better. She deserves anything but me. Cheeks burning with shame, I recoil from the bed, but Nathalie seizes my wrists almost violently, her eyes black as flotsam. We linger in this strange embrace, staring into each other. Then with a careful hand, she peels her nightgown up around her waist, the pale of her soft belly exposed.

"Are you sure?" I ask.

She nods. "What about the flask?"

"It's oil," I say. "To relax you."

"You mean knock me out?" She shakes her head. "I want to be awake."

I grip the knife tighter. "I've never done this with the person watching."

"Would you rather I look away?"

"No," I say, and make the first incision.

She doesn't tremble. Her gaze, curious and bright, follows my every movement. She's a voyeur for her own body. I paste on her skin, and each piece merges at once with mine. No waiting. No sleeping it off.

My body hums pleasantly, like I drank too much champagne, and I wander into the bathroom to rinse off the ugly parts of tonight. I try to rinse off Emily, though it doesn't take.

The shower curtain whispers behind me, and Nathalie steps into the tub. Her breath is warm against my back.

"May I touch?"

"Yes," I say.

Her fingers trace the outline of the transplanted flesh. She's close, so close, and I wish I could inhale her scent, the melody of her skin, but all I can smell is the acid stench of turpentine. Nathalie doesn't care. She pulls me into her and kisses my shoulders, my neck, my lips. I let her. In the dark, I pretend our skin is one. I pretend we're the same.

I pretend she's Emily.

※

The real Emily finds me at the downtown farmers' market on a Saturday morning. I'm picking up Swiss chard and kale for a stir-fry Nathalie wants to try tonight. We've become that couple, the one that prepares silly recipes clipped out of full-color magazines where the pictures are always prettier than what you cook. No more freeze-dried dinners for her. I want to make this evening special.

I'm sorting through a crate of leafy greens, so I don't notice the tingling in my skin or the spun sugar in my throat. By the time I look up, Emily has her hand on mine.

"Hey, darling," she says. "Where you been?"

My body stiffens, and I struggle to free my fingers from hers. "Nowhere special."

137

A lie. And a transparent one too. Emily smiles a serpent's smile.

"So you found yourself a regular?" She nudges me, like a horny teenager in a locker room. "It's the best, isn't it? How the layers of skin melt together like butter?"

I inch away from her, clutching an armful of soggy produce. "No," I say.

She raises an eyebrow. "No, it isn't good?"

"No, I don't have a regular."

I shuffle to the checkout, and Emily follows, her hand grasping for mine. For an instant, I taste copper, like a penny's caught beneath my tongue. Emily's jealous, and that scares me a little. Emily's never jealous.

I pay with a roll of quarters, and gather the brown paper bags.

"One more thing." Emily steps in front of me. "I want you to meet my fiancé."

She invites me to Sunday brunch the next day. I almost laugh at the absurdity of it—Emily with her quilted skin, sipping mimosas and dining on egg white omelets. As if she's normal. As if any of us are normal.

"We'll be at a table in the back," she says. "Noon sharp. Don't be late."

I watch her go, those beautiful bones shimmering beneath her skin. I want to drop these bags on the pavement and chase after her. I don't care where she goes. She could lead me into the bowels of hell, and I wouldn't mind.

At the corner, she grins back at me. "And feel free to bring someone," she says. "I'd love to meet her."

That night, the stir-fry is tasteless and dry.

"I'm sorry you didn't enjoy it," Nathalie says as she rinses the dishes. Her hands are raw and chapped from what I've done to her.

The next morning, I sneak out of bed early. "Business" is

all I tell her.

In a fancy new restaurant on the North Shore, the kind of place with bleached linens and pine-fresh floors, Emily waits for me, a gorgeous figure snuggled up in the booth next to her.

He's what I expect. Smiley and broad-shouldered, his lesion-spotted arm slung around her waist. Charming but dim. He would never suspect what she's doing to him.

When I sit down, she never says his name. I never ask. For the next hour, I chew tasteless fruit cocktail and listen to their meet-cute story retold again and again, enough to break my heart a hundred times. I don't know why I came here. I don't know why I let Emily invent new ways to hurt me.

After my third Bloody Mary, I excuse myself and head for the door, but Emily gets there first.

"Leaving already?" She smiles at me. "I thought we were friends, Clare."

Like Emily is friends with anyone.

"I need to go," I mutter.

"First, let me tell you something."

Emily presses her lips to my ear, and I smell turpentine on her skin.

"I'm pregnant," she says.

<hr/>

I feel every roil of morning sickness, every kick and contortion as the baby grows. I quit the coffeehouse and spend all day at the boardwalk, layering on Nathalie's skin, more and more to deaden the sound of Emily, but nothing works. I still taste sugar, cloying and artificial on my tongue. She's always with me.

"Is there anything I can do?" Nathalie asks when I can't sleep.

I shake my head and try not to stare at the pink patches

on her skin where I got greedy. Where I thought of Emily and dug the knife too deep.

At night, after her fiancé dreams, Emily wanders through downtown, calling for me.

Clare, darling. Where are you?

I close my eyes. I want to go to her, but it will always be the same. She's here and not here, haunting me like a ghost.

"I love you," Nathalie says, but I hear the words in Emily's voice.

※

I awaken to the sharp tang of blood filling my mouth. So much blood that I dry-heave over the bed. There's no liquid in my throat. It's Emily. Something's wrong.

I yank on my clothes, shirt inside-out and pants half-buttoned.

Nathalie drapes across the mattress, the sheets wadded up around her like a shroud. "Don't go." Her voice is frail and pitiful.

I pull on my boots. "I have no choice."

"Yes, you do," she says. "You don't need to run to her every time she calls."

My breath catches. I've never told her about Emily. I didn't have to. Nathalie sees through me, through this mass of skin to what I am beneath it all.

"I'm sorry," I say.

I trudge across town. Emily lingers barefoot in front of her apartment, her belly round as an Old World globe.

"There's been an accident," she says.

On the floor of the half-furnished nursery, her fiancé gapes blankly into the dark, seeing nothing. His blood pools around the cradle.

"The other girls came, but I sent them away." Emily wraps

her arms around my waist. "I only wanted you."

My heart in my throat, I vivisect him like a bullfrog, and we merge his flesh with ours. But we can't hide this like before. He's no stranger to her. Soon, people will come looking for him. They'll come looking for her, too.

"We need to leave," Emily says, and grasps my hand so tight my bones crack beneath the skin. "We'll start over. Just you and me."

I peer at her through the dim room. This could have been an accident, like she said. Cutting the wrong slice or at the wrong angle. It could happen to any of us.

Or maybe this was for me. His body shared between us. A sacrifice. This might be the only way Emily can say I love you.

She tells me to get my things and meet her at the bus station. At the doorway, I look back at her, and she smiles. For the first time, I can't see the outline of her bones. Emily has assumed the shape of so many people in her life that now she isn't anyone at all.

My body aches every step back to the boardwalk.

Nathalie waits up in bed, her eyes red from crying. "Are you okay?"

I nod, not looking at her.

She swallows the last of her tears. "Do you need anything, Clare?"

This is our cycle. She offers me what I want, and I take it. I'll carve her up, piece by piece until the night the blade inevitably slips. Then Nathalie will become no more than residue beneath my hide, a heinous evening ritual cataloged and forgotten.

And even if I leave with Emily tonight, anywhere we go, it will be the same. In this skin, I will be the same.

"No," I say. "I don't need anything."

Nathalie tugs the sheet up to her throat. "Come to bed."

"In a minute."

The knife is heavy in my hands as I retreat to the bathroom and turn on the shower. Hot water, full blast. The heat will make this easier. As if anything about this will be easy.

I shed my clothes and step into the tub. The water steams against my body. I pick a spot on my skin—any spot, it doesn't matter. This task requires no precision, no steady hand, nothing except a fool's willingness.

The work isn't what I expect. My hide isn't tough or immobile. The flesh never did fuse to my bones.

When I'm finished, my skin curls at my feet like an apple peeled in one long strip. It's inside out, and the first piece is exposed. I'm looking at my life in reverse. The earliest layer I can no longer remember. And the final layer I wish I could forget.

The shower cuts out, and water slides slowly down the slick of my bones. I sling my discarded flesh over my shoulder and shrug on Nathalie's robe, the oil and knife tucked in the pocket. The terrycloth fabric is rough against my body. Without a thick casing to protect me, everything is rough and strange.

Outside, on the crumbling boardwalk, the saltwater air chills my bones. Morning is brimming around the edges of the world, but daylight hasn't broken. I'm safe in the open for now. Even if a fisherman hums by on his boat, all he'll discern in the waning shadows of evening is the shape of a lonely girl on the shore. He won't see me for what I am—a cage of beautiful bones I've hidden too long beneath other people's promises.

But hiding was never my choice.

This is my choice.

In this place of long forgotten freak shows and dime-store illusions, I walk with the measured gait of a soldier to the end of the pier and toss my skin into the sea. It bobs on the waves before sinking beneath the dark water.

The knife follows, sheath and all, and I skip the flask across the waves like a river stone. The stench of turpentine is gone forever.

In a dingy Greyhound station downtown, Emily will know something's wrong. In her flesh, she'll feel it, and the other girls will feel it too. They won't know for sure what's become of me until the tides wash my skin to shore, after the fishes and the sharks throw back the scraps like garbage.

The horizon turns golden, and I realize what I should do. Take that last step and let this body fall into the gloom where it belongs. But diving into the deep would be too simple. Besides, if I change my mind tomorrow, the ocean will wait for me.

I steal into the bedroom, where Nathalie breathes as softly as a lullaby. I could still catch that bus. How Emily would scream if she saw me. How everyone in this town would scream. All the soccer moms and hipsters who used to snarl at me in the coffeehouse wouldn't snarl anymore. They'd cower before this body.

But I don't care about them.

The robe dances to the floor, and I crawl beneath the sheets. Nathalie murmurs in her dreams, and I edge closer, desperate to rest a few precious minutes before she awakens and discovers what I've become.

But the chill of my exposed bones rouses her from sleep, and she sits up, squinting at me in the darkness.

"Clare?"

For the first time, she sees me—the monster I've always been. I'm sure she'll scream. She'll shove me from this mattress, chase me from this bedroom, and deadbolt the door behind me.

And I won't blame her.

Her gaze slides up and down my body like the soft caress of fingertips. I hold my breath and shiver.

"You're cold," she whispers, and wraps the sheet tight around me before nestling against my body, our limbs tangled together, flesh against bone. She's warm and feels like a summer memory, like a dream from childhood long ago lost but now reclaimed.

The glint of dawn peeks through the boardwalk windows, and I bury my face against her, inhaling a clear breath at last.

Her skin's as sweet as honey.

BY NOW,
I'LL PROBABLY
BE GONE

B Y NOW, I'LL probably be gone.
Just so you know.

I love you.

That's the first thing.

Really, that's the only thing. There isn't much that matters more than you and me and all the secrets and all the laughs and all the silly rituals we used to share. Like how we'd sleep in on Sundays and get up at noon and make ourselves brunch in the kitchen, both of us still dressed in our old flannel pajamas.

What music would we listen to? Was it the Ramones?

(I was always so punk rock.)

Or your Gordon Lightfoot records?

(You were always so not-punk rock.)

I can't remember which it was now. Isn't that a shame how

the little details slip away? We hold on to the memories we don't want, and we lose the ones we cherish. Scientists should figure out a way to preserve happiness in a jar of formaldehyde, like that vivisected bullfrog we saw once at the Natural History Museum. Then we could smile all the time.

But who knows? Maybe that leathery frog under glass is the embodiment of happiness, and we haven't realized it yet, haven't realized how stasis is an underrated luxury.

(Did you realize it, and just not tell me? That would be like you, deciphering a secret of the universe but keeping it to yourself.)

❧

I want you to be happy.

That's the second thing.

A clichéd thing, I know. Don't all former lovers wish their old paramours happiness? Okay, the vengeful ones probably don't, but I try not to be vengeful.

(Was I vengeful? That wasn't my intention.)

❧

I never meant for it to go this far.

That's the third thing. Maybe the most important thing too, even more important than loving you.

(You already knew I loved you, right?)

Everything got away from me. I never intended to toss down the decanter on the kitchen tile when we were making buckwheat pancakes for dinner.

(Remember how we used to make breakfast for dinner? Weren't we a fun couple?)

But then I never intended to smell her perfume, as sweet as fresh honeysuckle, on the collar of your jacket.

146

Your face bloomed a thousand shades of red when I accused you, and I'll always remember the heavy footfalls when you stormed out of the apartment. When you went to meet her, one of your "late-night business meetings."

(Since when did they start calling it "business"?)

It was good you left when you did.

I wanted to hurt you.

(I couldn't hurt you.)

So I poured the pain into myself.

(What else could I do?)

The glass was already shattered on the floor. It didn't take much to find a vein.

(My blood on the tile looked thick as maple syrup. I faded out still thinking of dinner with you.)

❧

I don't want to stay here.

There are a hundred places we visited where I would prefer to be.

The Eiffel Tower, for one. Or how about the Redwood Forest? Even the trolley station down the block would be a welcome change. This apartment is uglier than I remember.

Garish lighting.

(How did I ever apply my makeup in such harsh fluorescents?)

And terrible company.

(I hear you whisper to her on the phone. You haven't changed a bit.)

I know you won't bring her here until you're sure it's safe. And as long as I keep zapping out the light bulbs in the hall and moaning the night before your big presentation at work, you're sure it's anything but safe.

(How charming of you to bring in that exorcist last week!

I haven't laughed like that since before those late-night business meetings of yours started last year!)

But don't worry. Even though your priest and his holy water didn't so much as tickle, I'll quiet down for now. I'll let you get some rest.

✥

And here's the last thing.

I might not leave at all.

I might wait here, pretending your exorcism drove me out.

(I couldn't hurt you once before.)

You'll think it's safe. You'll bring her into this place where you and I danced together, where we pretended to believe in forever.

(But I've learned a few things since then.)

You'll light a row of pink candles, just for her.

(Those were my candles, you know. My sister gave them to me last Christmas.)

And you'll take your lover, still sweet-scented like honeysuckle, to the bed that was ours—*is* ours.

But I'll be there too, twisted between the sheets.

She'll tell you the room's suddenly cold. You won't listen to her.

(You never were good at listening, were you?)

My body no more than a shadow, I'll wrap my fingers like ice around her pale throat and make you watch as I turn her blue.

Then, when you're dialing for help, I'll emerge, just for you, in the glow of candlelight.

Your scream will sound like a serenade.

The ambulance will wail, but all the best doctors and all the best nurses won't bring you back again.

You'll belong with me.

(Will we make a good family, the three of us?)

I bet you'll hate the lighting as much as I hate it.

(Does your lover like brunch, too?)

I bet you'll hate the company as well.

(Does she like to sleep until noon on Sundays?)

I bet you'll wish you were as lucky as that museum frog, splayed spread-eagle for the rest of time.

(Do you think eternity is long enough to earn forgiveness? Because I'm not so sure.)

※

By now, I'll probably be gone.

Unless, of course, I'm still here.

THROUGH EARTH AND SKY

IF THEY LISTENED, they'd know your people don't live in pointed tents. Some don't live at all, invisible like ghosts, reduced to kitschy feather knickknacks kept on mantles.

If they listened, they'd know you and your sister have no mantle or anything else besides a loan on a mattress that's more rust than springs and faded linens the color of urine. You don't even own the clothes on your back. The women do, the ones with tight-knit mouths and rulers always ready to smack wayward fingers. They own you as well as the other children who saw their parents vanish, dead before their time. That's the way it goes with people like you.

If they listened, they'd know you like magic, the same magic all kids share—secrets you keep, wishes you make, silly incantations you recite to the darkness where no one can hear.

But here inside these walls, where lonely children live, you aren't supposed to care about spells or magnetic sand or dreamcatchers in windows. Magic can't be yours. That's what the unsmiling women tell you.

"Besides," they say, "it's a cliché that your people like magic. You don't want to be a cliché, do you?"

Yet magic is all you have.

If they listened, they'd know what happens when children have nothing else. What they do have becomes more powerful, more potent than it would be in a happy child's hands, a child with two parents and a pretty house and a baby doll that cries 'Mama.' You and your sister have no baby dolls, but you have each other, and together, your words, your wishes, your secrets become real. A sunny day when you say so. A ruler broken in two before it reaches your cheeks. Little things, insignificant things, the only things that matter.

Soon you grow older and can't recall what your childhood secrets were, but the wind remembers for you. The wind is your companion, and it never turns you away. It always listens.

And the wind is a good listener.

If they listened, they'd know why two girls with no family except each other marry the first men who will have them. The cruel women give you no other choice, but matrimony brings a different kind of rules and rulers. In this mining town, faces and hands and men become hard and weathered, and the black ash of West Virginia blankets everything, inside and out.

On your wedding day, you can hardly see the men's faces—they're caked too thick with dirt and dust. Not even your magic can fix that.

If they listened, they'd know love cannot be captured in a potion, no matter how hard you try, and when your hair is a gloss of black and skin a perfect copper, love will only come after years of marriage, if it comes at all. Even once they claim they love you, the men won't let you forget how you're lucky to have them, lucky to bask in the glow of their pale skin, however sullied from years of work. Being near them will make you whiter, won't it?

If they listened, they wouldn't wave you off when you rail against your sister's husband.

"He goes to work, day after day," they say, "and that's enough."

But the glint in his eye—that wandering eye—says it's not enough, not when he quaffs a bottle of cheap whiskey instead of bringing home his pay, not when that whiskey boils inside him, coursing through his veins like fire, not when he raises his hand to your only sister and brings it down again and again until her skin is a tapestry of welts.

Together, your magic could overwhelm him, but she won't make a wish against her husband.

"I'm his wife," she says. "I can't betray him."

If they listened, they'd try to help you.

But they don't listen. Only the man you loathe notices you, how the wind wraps around you as you fill your sister's pockets with smoky quartz, desperate to protect her.

"Witch," her husband says, and you smile.

If they listened, they'd know magic is imperfect. Sometimes, it fails, especially when a spell needs two. And you no longer have two. Your sister disappears into the night without a word. There is no body. He hides it well. The hills of West Virginia hide it for him.

"He did this to her," you tell them, but they don't listen. She's just another tally mark, vanished with the rest, dead before her time. The way it goes with people like you.

If they listened, those with the fine carriages and finer lace, they'd know justice is more than a gavel and a courtroom and a man yelling 'Order!' Here in your house no more than a shack, justice is a pot on a stove and the remnants of a chicken. You ate the meat last week, but that doesn't mean the leftovers—the blood and the bones—can't still do some good.

If they listened, they'd know the recipe you use to raise your sister's bones, bring her through earth and sky, bring her home to you. While your husband and children dream their lazy dreams, her bones sit with you at the rickety hand-me-down table. Her bones tell you secrets. These are secrets you and she will never forget.

Her husband runs because he knows those secrets are no longer safe. After all, a witch can't be trusted.

If they listened, they'd know magic pays distance no mind. It doesn't take long for the wind to find him, and a little bit at a time, his ulcerated guts tie into knots. He must suffer as you suffer, slowly and without end. At night, you can hear him scream over blue-green mountains and valleys built from coal and sweat.

If they listened, they could hear him too. But they don't listen, and this time, it's probably good. Because if they heard him scream and knew you were to blame, they'd burn you on the nearest pyre.

If they listened, they'd know you leave that mining town. Your husband earns a good job by the sea, and while you'll miss those hills that brought your sister back to you, albeit for one night, you won't miss the stink of death and the cinders that permeate everyone and everything there. Before you leave, you drive past the building, the prison, where you and your sister stayed as kids. It's converted to offices now.

If they listened, they'd know your children grow and have children of their own, but your mind never strays far from the place you left behind. Where others smell the salt of the ocean, you can remember only the acrid stench of smog. Your sister should be here with you instead of in the earth where you laid her bones. She rests but you cannot. The wounds inside you never close.

Far away, her husband's guts remain in knots, but his life continues, and he eyes another young wife whose face his fists will mar. He never changes, so you must be the one to change him. It is your duty to protect those like your sister, those who can't protect themselves. You muster every bit of magic left in you and ask the wind to cross a thousand miles. A stalwart friend, it obliges. Her husband screams out a final time and then retreats to silence even blacker than coal. The past is bones now and nothing more. In your fine house, no longer a shack, you recline in your rocking chair, smiling to yourself. At last, you feel complete—or as complete as you'll ever be without your sister. Your partner in magic lost forever.

But a new partner is waiting, his chestnut eyes staring up at you.

If they listened, they'd know about your grandson. Whenever he misbehaves, you laugh and put the evil eye on him, your gaze narrowed, your gnarled hands suspended in the air, but you don't scare him. He just giggles and scurries away. It never occurs to him how strange it is his grandmother's a witch. He accepts it like the wind and the sun and the color of your hair—bolts of nighttime hidden inside the gray. His grandmother is gray and she is a witch. These things are the same in his eyes, and neither one is wrong.

If they listened, they'd know that little boy with the ornery grin gives you hope. You watch him speak to trees. You watch the wind protect him. You protect him too, but you won't always be here. The earth and the sky will, and they'll care for him well.

If they listened, they'd know all these things and more, a world beyond, so much greater than them and greater than you. But they don't listen. And they never will.

Your secrets remain with the wind.

THE
TOWER
PRINCESSES

E VERYBODY KNOWS A tower princess.
She might be the daughter of a friend of a friend. Or the girl next door who hides behind drawn blinds. Sometimes, she's no more than an urban legend, like Bloody Mary, alive only when kids whisper about her late at night after their parents retire to bed.

Tower princesses aren't as exotic as they sound. They aren't really royalty. They aren't really anything. Just girls living in regular neighborhoods with mothers and fathers and a sibling or two. Plain as can be, or at least as plain as every other girl in the world.

As plain as me.

Except for the tower.

✻✻✻

I'm a senior in high school when the government hands down a special mandate in the princesses' honor. Something about expanding accessibility requirements in hopes of preventing isolation. The princesses are nothing if not isolated. Parents tip them sideways and hide them in basements and attics, because what else are you going to do with a girl in a nine-foot tower?

Madeline's Law, the government calls the new directive, named after a princess who hanged herself from her own turret after her family abandoned her in the backyard shed with a running hose and a bowl of Wonder Bread crusts.

Nobody knows how she got the rope.

Nobody cares either. The parents and administrators are more concerned about the princesses joining regular classrooms.

"Why can't they be homeschooled?" my mother asks in a town hall meeting. "I'm sure the girls would be happier that way."

Everyone with an opinion is certain they know what's best for the tower princesses.

⚜

A tower is like a fingerprint. Each one is slightly different. Different materials, different heights. Some are built of brass, others of mahogany, or redwood. The worst are barbed wire or rose thorns and cut the princesses if they move too fast or some bozo bumps into them in the hallway or lunch line. The school creates a strict policy about reinforcing the outsides of towers to render them harmless to passing students, but nobody's too worried about what happens inside.

Even the highest towers don't look like towers. They're more akin to moving coffins, birdcages with solid walls instead of thin copper bars, never taller than a dozen feet and just wide enough for the princesses to stand, perfectly postured at all times.

At night, while my parents and brother snore in the next

rooms, I curl in my bed, knees tucked into my chest, and wonder how the princesses sleep.

❧

By the end of September, seven tower princesses enroll at our school. Their first day, the teachers don't ask them to introduce themselves.

"Best to ignore them," they say. "The sooner they realize this isn't where they belong, the better."

But I can't ignore them. At least not the girl in my grade. She's different than the others. Her scent reminds me of an orchid in bloom. We share almost every class, and whenever she's nearby, my head spins, and my bones turn liquid, like mercury flowing freeform inside me.

At five-and-a-half feet, her tower is shorter than the rest, but it's strong. Made of titanium, I hear the teachers whisper. Smooth and polished, the color of simmering charcoal. She bumps into me in the hall after geometry, and the cold metal against my skin is like a shock of blue electricity. It doesn't hurt, not really, but I jump back on instinct, and a mountain of math and social studies textbooks spills from my arms.

"Pardon me," says a voice, tinny and distant, inside the tower.

"It's fine," I say.

A guy at the next locker groans. "One of them touched you. You're *infected* now."

He says it loud enough for the girl in titanium to hear as she shuffles to her next class.

"Leave her alone," I mutter.

I hate the boys. Out in the open, they taunt the princesses, but anytime they think no one's looking, they paw at the towers like rabid wolves. That's how I see them—with glistening fangs and a steady stream of drool dripping down their chins.

159

They're always circling their prey, searching for weaknesses.

The boys are dangerous, though the teachers never listen when I speak up.

"Those young men come from good families," they say, as if blue blood lineage precludes bad behavior.

After school, the boys gather out front to watch and cat-call the girls, so I shortcut out the back, past Carol's 24-Hour Diner where the waitresses wear funny pink hats, and down the alley behind Joe's Butcher Shop.

Nobody sees me. I'm in an invisible tower, one that shuts me off from the world. I could wander for hours. Provided my chores are done, my family never notices I'm missing.

At the city limits, I trudge among a scrawny forest. Most of the trees were trimmed years ago to make way for power lines and sewage grates, but a few willows, emerald and withering, survived. I settle in the dirt and scribble messages in my notebook to the wind and the rain.

How are you? Where do you come from? Where do you go?

With a careful hand, I tuck the letter in the carved hollow of the tallest tree.

This becomes my new favorite thing. Slinking out the back door at school and coming here. Especially since each time I return, my message is gone.

I tell myself the wind swallows the paper, or a mama bird stuffs my handwriting in her nest as fodder.

That's the lie I believe.

Until the day I get a note back.

❧

The girls aren't born in towers. The towers show up later, typically around fifth or sixth grade. Not much can predict which girl will get a tower and which won't. People with clipboards and fancy diplomas slanted on walls are always trying to pinpoint it, inspecting the data for correlations in socioeconomic status or mental health, but it's all spurious, and nothing in the research pops.

A normal girl, a weird girl, a rich girl, a poor girl. Anybody's fair game for a tower.

So long as you're a girl.

※

Each day, in the cafeteria, the princesses cluster in small groups, and an aide feeds them through the narrow slit in their walls. Each tower has one gap near the top, a window for nourishment and waste removal, and all the boys guffaw and makes jokes about what they'd do with that opening if given the chance.

"I'd make those girls scream my name," my brother Sam says, and kicks up his dirty feet on the kitchen table.

Sam's feet are always dirty. Dirty as his mind, I say.

I keep my head down at the sink and clean our dishes from dinner. My brother doesn't do dishes. Our mother says it's my job.

Sam leans closer to me, his chair balanced on one leg, and pinches my waist.

I yip.

"Admit it, Mary," he says. "You fantasize about getting your fingers up inside one of them, don't you?"

Our mother, laundry basket in tow, peeks around the corner. "What was that I heard about fingers and towers?"

"Nothing," Sam says, shoving his hands in his pockets.

After I finish at the sink, I creep to my room and reread the message from the willow. It's written on green paper in the most beautiful calligraphy I've ever seen.

Hello. How are you?

I smile and memorize every curve of the handwriting. By

161

the end of the evening, I've folded and unfolded the note so many times it disintegrates between my fingers.

❧

The school initially plans a special classroom for the tower princesses, with peaked ceilings and broad doors and an entrance at the far end of the building where they can't bother the rest of us. But then a federal inspector comes and nixes that idea, saying no, no, no, nothing to segregate them. The law, he reminds the principal, dictates the girls must mix with the other students.

This is not welcome news. In their monthly newsletter, the teachers claim in vehement and colorful terms that the tower princesses pose an exceptional health risk to others.

These girls lack any discernible coordination, and given their towers' colossal weight and size, they could crush your son or daughter in an integrated classroom!

Bold print doesn't lie, my mother always says when she reads their latest drivel. And it is true the girls have a problem with balance. Hard to be graceful when you can't properly stretch your legs. A few princesses have sawed small holes in the bottoms of their towers, so they can wiggle their feet through and walk on their own, but even then, they're top heavy and have a tendency to tip.

Crushed! Your son or daughter will be CRUSHED!

The other girls need constant transportation, in the form of electronic platforms, which are basically scooters, only wider and with less color options.

Should your taxpayer dollars go to supporting the transport of someone who is a hazard to your child's health? We surely don't think so!

During French IV, I'm seated near the girl in the titanium tower. As always, she makes my skin buzz.

"Up late?" she whispers, but I pretend not to hear her.

She's right though. Last night, I fell asleep at the willow, hopeful I'd discover the person leaving me notes. No luck.

The teacher passes out an exam, and I hunch over the blank spaces where my English translations should go.

Souhaiter. Vouloir. Adorer.

I don't know any of these terms. This is a failing grade. I'm seventeen and can't pass a basic vocab quiz.

My cheeks burn, and I clench my jaw to hold back tears. Next to me, the princess is watching. I can feel her gaze sear through me like wildfire. I'm curious what she sees.

She lurches within her tower—maybe because she's restless, maybe to get my attention—and the tips of her turrets crack the classroom wall. The pipes inside fracture, and sewage spurts onto our desks.

And even sitting still, these girls are a distraction, and let's face it: they rarely sit still.

We're immediately evacuated for the day. Biohazard, the teacher says. Later, when I'm studying for the retake exam, I almost wonder if the girl did it on purpose.

To save me.

⚜

Cutting open a tower to extract a princess sounds like a reasonable solution, and sometimes, well-meaning parents give it a try, but it never takes. The tower always grows back. The towers are alive and feral and don't easily surrender what is theirs.

So we leave the girls as they are, prisoners in plain sight.

"It's safer this way," the adults say. "Nobody can hurt them if they're all locked up."

I think of this, the shelter of a tower, the day a group of senior boys knock me down in the alley behind Joe's Butcher Shop and tear the buttons off my silk blouse. I'm headed to my willow tree, another note written and tucked in my pocket.

I don't make it to the forest. Not today.

These boys with football muscles and laughs like retching hyenas remove their cell phones and record what they do to me, the kicking and spitting and roving hands, their fingertips pressing into my flesh as though I'm made of pudding. They want all of me, a body not swathed in a tower but free and open for the taking, and they want to hear me scream and beg them to stop.

But what they don't know is I can kick and spit and use my hands too. I scratch the biggest of the boys, the leader, because I hope if he falls, the others might follow. I go for his eyes, and he thrashes and whines and falls to his knees, screaming for his mother.

Boys are apparently more delicate than they look. Maybe they'd do better if they could hide in towers too.

The ambulance arrives like a wailing banshee, and though I'm clutching the tattered remains of my clothes across my claw-marked breasts, the paramedics service the injured boy first, spiriting him to the hospital where he stays for a week. His parents try to bill my parents for the care, but since one of the boys was fool enough to put the back alley escapade on YouTube, we don't pay a single penny.

But the case never gets to court. Everyone says that's for the best, that I would never have held up on the stand, not when a brigade of Armani-suited Ivy League lawyers were out for my flesh. Besides, the cops remind me, the boys didn't really *have* me, didn't make me bleed, not from the place that counts, so the incident goes down as a simple prank taken too far.

At home, my parents banish me to my bedroom, my father gritting his teeth and my mother sobbing.

"Why were you walking that way alone?" they ask again and again. "Why do you always cause us problems?"

I have no answer for them, so I stare at my shoes and wish

I was someone else.

After they've gone to bed, I climb through my window and head to the forest, keeping clear of the butcher shop.

A note is waiting in the willow.

I heard what happened. Are you okay?

No is all I write back.

I don't go home. Instead, I nestle in the cool earth and dream about those towers and those princesses and how nobody hurts them. How they're safe.

Safer than me anyhow.

⁂

When a tower grows around a princess, it happens overnight. One day, the girls are running and laughing and splashing in summer sprinklers, their bare feet slick against the grass. Then— bam! They awaken to find themselves locked up in a cage that moves, for good and all.

Because everybody knows once you're a tower princess, you never go back.

⁂

Things at school are worse than before. Things are always worse for girls who fight back.

Nobody trusts me now, not the teachers or the other students or even my own parents.

"You couldn't have humiliated Mom and Dad more if you'd birthed a tower," Sam says, chuckling.

In spite of the video, plenty of people claim I set up the whole thing.

"She's so desperate for attention," the girls with blond ponytails and pretty pink cheeks say. "Like any guy would want her."

165

Between classes, I duck outside to the chain link fence where the smokers hang. I've never had a cigarette in my life, but today, it's quiet here. And empty, except for the girl in the titanium tower.

"Hey, you," she says, and the white rays of the sun shine through the slit in the tower, revealing two eyes, green as a dew-draped meadow.

"Hey, me, *what?*" I say because I can't think of anything clever.

"I'm Linnea," she says. "You're Mary, right?"

She watches me as if I'm glass, and she can see inside me.

I wish I could see inside her too.

I shrug. "Yeah, I'm Mary. So what?"

"Could you do me a favor, Mary?"

I shouldn't do favors, especially favors for tower princesses. But Linnea's different. So I sneak a Pall Mall out of my mom's purse, and the next day, between fifth and sixth period, I light the end and fit it through the gap in the tower.

"Thank you, Mary." Linnea puffs out gray circles, and the tower looks like it's burning. "Want to share?"

I roll my eyes. "Whatever."

"Come here," she says, and I move close to her, so close the chill of the metal prickles my skin.

Our faces align through the tower. She leans forward and presses her lips to mine.

The smoke snakes down my throat, and I inhale. Everything turns sweet like caramel crystallizing on my tongue.

Linnea pulls away to catch her breath. Then she giggles and does it again. There's no smoke this time. Just a long, aching kiss.

When the bell rings, I sleepwalk to class, my life cleaved in two—before this moment, and after. And I can only think one thing.

I want more.

❋

After school, I leave another note at the willow. It's short, but it's my favorite message so far.

I met someone. She's beautiful.

I laugh, because how do I know if Linnea's beautiful? I've never seen her whole face at once. She's a mosaic, and I have to cobble together the pieces.

We meet at the chain link fence every day. She stops requesting cigarettes. She doesn't need an excuse to kiss me now.

"Have you ever done this before?" she asks.

I feel my cheeks flush. "Why does it matter?"

Her lips curl into a grin. "So you're almost eighteen, and I'm your first?"

"Don't make fun," I say.

She kisses me again, softer and sweeter this time.

Am I your first? I want to ask. But I don't. If she has kissed someone else, I'll drive myself crazy with the details—the who and the when and the where.

Better to focus on right now. Me and her. In the moments between, the moments without her, I'm holding my breath and waiting.

We're only safe when we're together.

❋

The school reports in December how the tower princesses are making good progress, but it's a lie. The boys still cajole them, and the teachers invent every excuse to exclude them.

"They can't toss a basketball or lob a volleyball, so what's the point of them taking gym?" the PE instructor says. "Send them to study hall instead."

So I'm far from Linnea when the blond ponytailed girls

167

shove me down in the shower after class. I strike my head on the mildewed tile, and they spit on me while I bleed.

It takes an hour for maintenance to discover me, and by then, my fingers are pruning and my skin's chapped raw beneath the heavy water the girls left to run after they skittered off to biology and algebra.

At the emergency room, the doctors poke and prod me.

"A week of bed rest," they say, and I know what that means.

No walks to the willow. No chain link fence between classes. And no Linnea.

I recline in bed for seven days and wish I was like her. I wish I was in a tower, so no one—not my parents or my brother or the mocking boys and girls—could ever put their hands on me again.

I envy the princesses. And I hate them a little too.

Except Linnea.

I could never hate her.

❧

When a princess dies, her family buries her in the tower. It's convenient, for sure, but there's no other choice. Upon her final breath, the tower calcifies around her.

Even in death, the tower protects the princess.

❧

It's the end of January when my parents find out about Linnea. My father hauls me out of bed and wallops me in the mouth so hard my lip splits.

"Is it true?" he asks, but it's clear he's already made up his mind.

My mother wilts in the doorway, sniveling like a Freudian hysteric on a fainting couch.

168

"See what you've done," my father says and tightens his grip around me. "Haven't you caused us enough problems without getting involved with one of those awful girls?"

"Way to go, Mary," Sam says as he saunters down the hallway. "I'm not watching this shit. I'm going out."

"Be safe," our mother says as my father raises his hand to me again.

I'm bruised and bandaged when Sam returns after midnight and climbs on top of me in my bed. He's been drinking cheap gin, and I gag down the taste of rotten pine needles on his breath.

He cups his hand over my mouth, so I won't scream.

"I bet you enjoyed what those boys did to you." He digs his fingers deep into the flesh of my thighs. "Maybe you'll enjoy it again too. Might set you right. Then you'd stay away from that girl."

Glistening teeth. Drool down his chin. Even my brother is a wolf.

I flail once and strike Sam's face. He coughs blood on my comforter, and I roll off the mattress and scramble for the door.

My shoes in hand, I dash to the willow, the town dissolving around me as I run. Everything is smears of color—the high school, the diner, the alley I avoid behind the butcher shop.

The forest. I need to reach the forest. It will protect me. I hold my breath until I'm concealed beneath the drooping fingers of the trees.

It's the middle of the night, but I'm not alone. Linnea's here.

And she's outside of her tower.

The world turns solid again, and I gape at her. "You can leave?"

She fidgets next to her titanium sarcophagus. "Sure, I can."

A green note dangles from her fingers, and her cheeks redden.

"I followed you once from school," she says. "Saw you leave

a message to the tree. Thought I'd write back."

"You lied to me," I say.

"No lying." She sniffs in the bitter air. "I would have told you. If you'd asked."

I sigh, and my breath blossoms in a plume of mist around me. "Who else knows?"

She shakes her head. "Nobody."

"Except me," I say.

"Except you."

She smiles, and I see her face, unadorned in the bare moonlight.

My message was right. She is beautiful.

I tell her about my parents and my brother, and she kisses the gash in my lips. This is our first kiss, the first one that counts, since at last I can run my fingers through her hair and rest my forehead against hers.

"How long can you stay gone?" I ask.

"Not sure," she says. "Maybe forever."

Maybe forever.

Maybe not forever.

An hourglass flipped upside down, and time is slipping away.

I take her hand, and we run. Through the trees and the streets and into the alley behind the butcher shop. I'm unafraid now, because Linnea's here with me, and together, we're impervious to pain.

In this moment, she is all things, and her jagged pieces fit into the curves of my jagged pieces, and the two of us, these broken girls, are whole for the first time.

She laughs, and I laugh, and this gray town overflowing with darkness laughs too.

Linnea leads me into the diner, and we sit side by side in a corner booth, drinking coffee and giggling at the pink hats the waitresses wear.

"You'd look quite fetching in one of those," she says and traces her fingers along the slope of my neck.

We kiss, and the waitress grunts at us to stop, but we don't care. This night belongs to us.

I ask Linnea how she can leave her tower.

"Parents have tried to cut girls out before," I say. "It never works."

"They take us out against our will." She quaffs what remains of her lukewarm coffee, imprinting the white ceramic mug with a pink lipstick kiss. "It's different if we leave voluntarily. The tower's a second skin. It protects us if we want it."

I inspect her face. "And what if you don't want it?"

She smiles. "Then it doesn't want us either."

Doesn't want her. How could anything not want her?

At dawn, the waitress kicks us out of the diner, and we return to the forest. Though the sun is piercing the edges of the trees, it's colder than we left it. We shiver next to the willow, and I memorize Linnea's silhouette, backlit by the crimson cast of the horizon.

"I can't go back home," I say. "Why don't we leave? Just you and me."

Linnea sighs, her gaze not meeting mine. "But where would we go? How would we get there? There's nowhere else for us."

She climbs inside her tower, and the edifice closes around her, like blood oozing over wire stitches. If we entwined our bodies, we could both fit inside the tower. We could be together and never worry about the outside world again.

But that's not what Linnea wants.

I swallow a ragged breath. "Why go back?"

"This is where I live, Mary," she says.

Where she lives. And where do I live? With a mom and dad and brother who always devise new ways to hurt me.

Rage, like a cancer, rises up my throat. I hate her. I hate

how she can choose, and I can't.

"You have everything," I say. "Safety when you want it. Freedom when you don't. And here I am, with nothing."

"You have more than nothing," Linnea whispers, her voice brittle in the night air. "You have me. I love you, Mary."

"Love?" I laugh once, a harsh laugh that ricochets off the sky. "As if love's enough."

I turn and walk away, pretending.

I pretend I don't see the tears in her eyes.

I pretend I don't hear her calling my name.

And most of all, I pretend I don't love her too.

※

We finish out twelfth grade, but we don't talk again. No walks to the willow. No detours to the fence. Linnea's less than a stranger to me now.

My parents smile over the dinner table.

"We're glad that phase is over," they say.

"Over," I echo.

I lock my bedroom door at night, so Sam can't get at me, and I count the days until I'm eighteen and can run from this place.

On the last day of school, I'm emptying my locker when Linnea finds me.

Her lithe fingers hold a note through the gap in her tower. "I put this in the tree nook," she says, "but I guess you aren't checking anymore."

After she vanishes down the hall, I unfold the green paper. It's sweet-scented and inscribed with those perfect cursive letters.

You win. We'll go. Meet me at midnight.

I scoff and shove the message in my bag. This is exactly what I want. Us against the universe. We could leave tonight and never look back.

But I still ache from before, from her not protecting me when I needed her, and I want her to ache like me.

So I'm an hour late to the willow. I assume she'll wait forever.

I'm wrong.

Next to the tree, the tower's there, but Linnea is gone.

I pace the forest, my face sweat-caked in the cold spring night, and weep her name. She never answers. Tears clogging my throat, I grapple with the willow, desperate to uncover a final note, a clue to where she went.

Linnea left nothing behind except the tower.

I climb inside her empty shell as if I'll find her hiding there, but all that remains is the ghost of distant orchids.

※

The years collapse in on themselves like a crumpled ball of scrap paper destined for the wastebasket. I squander a decade working every dead-end job in this town, never straying far from the city limits, never willing to surrender the memory of her.

I'm at the diner now, arrayed in a funny pink hat, serving customers at the same corner table where Linnea and I giggled a lifetime ago.

Everybody's forgotten about the girl in the titanium tower. They found her shell in the woods—where I left it, a souvenir too heavy to carry on my back. They launched no search. Nobody would know what to look for. Only I saw her face.

A few tower princesses stuck around after graduation. I see them at the grocery store with their families or strolling past the diner at night.

I wonder if they can leave their towers too.

I wonder if it even matters.

When I was young, I thought they got everything. I didn't realize we were the same—us girls who were blamed and mocked and disregarded.

My mother calls every day, leaving messages about my brother's latest arrest or my father's waning health, but I don't answer. After all these years and all this damage, I have nothing to say.

I shouldn't stay in this town. It's lonely and haunted. But this is my choice. To wait.

And to hope.

On my thirtieth birthday, I walk to the willow with one last note.

I love you. I've always loved you. Please forgive me.

The paper is yellowed and fragile as antique moth wings. These are the words I wrote the night Linnea vanished, but until today, I couldn't return here. Not after how I failed her.

The next morning, the ground is trampled, and the note is gone.

Of course, it could have drifted away in the faintest of breezes. Or an ambitious magpie might have stolen it for a May nest.

Or Linnea might have come back to reclaim what is—and always has been—hers.

I tell myself she'll come to me.

On a night I'm closing at the diner, the scent of orchids will waft through the kitchen, and I'll look to the swinging door and see that familiar outline.

She'll shimmy up to the counter and ask for a menu.

I'll give her one. I'll give her anything she wants.

She'll request only coffee.

Customers will wave at me, calling for their eggs over easy and their greasy hash browns, but I won't see them.

I'll only see her face, a roadmap of where she's been,

etched in paths around eyes and lips. The moments we missed together. The moments we could still have.

She'll linger at the counter until the others leave, disgruntled, and we're alone.

I'll flip the open sign to closed and lock the front door.

"Hey, you," she'll say at last, and my cheeks will burn like wildfire.

"Hey, me, *what*?" I'll ask because I can't think of anything clever.

Then she'll smile.

And so will I.

AND HER
SMILE WILL
UNTETHER
THE UNIVERSE

YOU DISCOVER HER first film by accident. It's the midnight
movie on a Saturday night cable access program, and since
it's horror, you leave it on for background noise. She receives
above-the-title billing along with a fancy "And Introducing"
credit, written in neat cursive letters. You vaguely remember
her name, though you don't know why. She appears in four
paltry scenes, and most of her screen time is spent screaming
and fleeing the monster, a hulking Karloff imitator arrayed in
green Ben Nye greasepaint caked too thick around his ears. A
waste of her talent, perhaps, but she's still mesmerizing.

You don't sleep that night. Instead you scour message
boards and defunct film blogs for every piece of trivia about
her. At the time of the film's release, the press reviews from
places like Variety said the same thing: "She's a real star; a true
discovery."

It's strange to think of her that way—in present tense.
She's been dead almost half a century now, turned to ash a full
ten years before you were born. There was no overlap between

the two of you. She was in the world. Pause. Then you were in the world.

But that's the thing about films. To them, there is no past. There's only the here and now. Celluloid might yellow, but the performers are always waiting for you.

She's always waiting.

On the screen, she glows and glides and never seems fettered to the earth. It would be easy to call her beautiful, but you think that word is generic, too one-size-fits-all, and besides, her beauty isn't what sticks with you. Her voice is what you remember most: low and clear and otherworldly, like she's already speaking from beyond the grave, from somewhere far and near at the same time.

This is the only film where she used that voice, which leads to suspicion among bored bloggers who write about obscure cinema.

No way is that her real voice.

She never sounded like that in her other movies or interviews.

Totally dubbed. And badly dubbed too.

This makes your guts burn, the way they deny her. She spent three months with a speech coach, singing scales and repeating tongue twisters like "red leather, yellow leather" until her mouth went numb, but these bloggers must not know that, they must not have researched her like you have. Or maybe they figure she was just a pretty face, and everybody knows pretty faces don't understand a thing about hard work.

Her first film isn't a good film, but it's one of her only films, so you buy a copy on eBay and watch it over and over. She made four movies in total—five if you include the grainy footage shot on Super 8 in her house that final night.

You don't want to watch that one. You don't want to see what they do to her, those monsters hiding in plain sight.

There are no monsters in her second film. It's a psychedelic music movie featuring a band no one remembers with songs everyone would rather forget. Catchy little pop ditties that grate at the air and make you wish you didn't have ears at all.

She plays a groupie who's in love with the lead singer, and her voice is indeed different, more high-pitched but never shrill, every word lilting and lovely as a cathedral bell at midnight. "Hypnotic" is how *Panorama Magazine* described her performance.

As part of the film's release, the studio produced a promotional album that included a few extra songs, as though one bad tune deserved another three. You don't think much of this until your hipster film buff friends bring it up at brunch one Sunday.

"You've never heard the urban legend?" they ask, and you roll your eyes, since you wouldn't be asking if you had.

In faux-hushed voices like kids at a Ouija board, they tell you that if you hit play on the film at the same time as you drop the needle on the vinyl, the two sync up, sort of like *The Wizard of Oz* and *Dark Side of the Moon*, but not exactly.

"This is way spookier," they promise.

You don't believe them, but you agree to let them come over to your apartment, mostly because you can't find the film on Netflix, and they already own a bootleg. They drink all your beer and start on the whiskey and vodka stored beneath your bathroom sink, but you don't argue. Thanks to them, you'll see her tonight.

She doesn't come in until halfway through the film. On the dusty turntable, the speakers crackle with a song titled "In a Devil's Eye." You suddenly can't breathe.

"Here it is," your friends say, and you hush them, because this is a hallowed moment. She's on screen, and it's a close-up.

With her eyes downcast, she steps forward, as if she's walking toward you. Your heart tugs tight like a stone in your chest, as the sunlight hits her face just right. Her skin shimmers, a strange shift that doesn't look confined to the screen. It looks like it's happening somewhere in the middle, between where she is and where you are.

She turns to you, and she flashes a ghost of a smile, a secret shared between the two of you.

She sees you. You know she does.

Then she looks away, and the moment is lost.

And no matter how many times you rewind it, she'll only do it once.

So pay attention.

⁂

On the set of her third film, she met the love of her life, the man she would have married if she hadn't been sliced up like prosciutto first. They were bohemian and boisterous, frequenting all the best parties and nightclubs of the era, the Studio 54s and Playboy Clubs and Annabel's in Berkeley Square. He wore ascots, and she wore crinoline, and they were almost too fabulous for the camera to bear.

They play a couple in this film, a Gothic story set in the English moors, and you can practically watch them fall in love on-screen. You scowl at him every time he gallops into the frame on his white stallion. You know from biographies that he cheated on her almost as soon as they met, and that he married another, less deceased ingénue only six months after she died.

But you mostly hate him because she loved him, and she never loved you.

When you watch this film, you're by yourself. You pretend you don't want to hear the snarky commentary of your too-clever friends or deal with them drinking all the Sierra Nevada Pale Ale and eating all the takeout lo mein, but that's not the real reason. The real reason is that you want to be alone with her.

180

It's ridiculous. It's the truth.

In the film, she plays a woebegone maiden, and her would-be husband is a brooding landowner, who harbors a secret too terrible to reveal until the climax. You expect it will be a wife in the attic, and of course, it is.

By the last scene, you're half asleep, trying not to doze because that would be rude. She's a marvelous actress, after all, with her wistful looks and soft-spoken dialogue, but like the first two films, this one isn't very good. In spite of yourself, your eyes blear out and then clear, and when you blink, she's looking right at you again, just like during the last film, but this time, the moment doesn't flicker away. Your stomach twists, and you sit up in your chair. She holds your stare, and you hold hers as you wet your lips and wait, breathless for what she'll do next.

Her hand unsteady, she reaches toward the screen and breaks the fourth wall. The whole apartment shakes, and your feet lift out from under you, the world spinning into darkness.

When you open your eyes, you're lying spread-eagled on the other side of the room. This neither surprises nor bothers you. If anything, it excites you. Nobody warned you about this. Is it another urban legend your hipster friends never mentioned, or was this meant for you alone?

You peel yourself off the floor and run the film back. The scene isn't there anymore. Once again, you're not surprised, but you are—even if you don't want to admit it—a touch disappointed.

You finish what's left of the third film—as expected, the estate with the silly name burns to the ground, and everybody laments—but that night, you can't sleep. She'll haunt you now. She'll live in your veins, not like a disease or a poison, but like a cure.

You'll want to pull her out of the screen, to rewrite history and bring her back as gleaming and perfect as she was before.

Or better yet, you'll want to crawl right through the cigarette burns, into the spaces between the frames. You'll want to go where she is. Even if that place is dark and yawning and packed with earth, six feet deep.

You squeeze your eyes closed, and for reasons you can't quite understand, tears seep down your cheeks. You steady your breath, and you promise yourself that somehow, you'll save her.

And she'll save you.

※

Though it isn't horror, the fourth film is the ghastliest of the bunch, a cheesy cult classic with highbrow fashion and lowbrow dialogue. She had to say things like "Oh, baby, don't worry. Marla Doll is here now!" and keep a straight face. But she said it, and said it well, every syllable enunciated with the commitment of a Shakespearean pro. By this film, her voice is steadier, more confident. She was coming into her own, a prime that would never be realized.

All the bloggers talk about this film, not because it's good, but because of the behind-the-scenes story. Her killers sneaked onto the set. Of course, they weren't her killers then. They were merely strangers to her, hyena-laughing hippies that weren't really hippies at all. Hippies were in it for the peace and love. These four were in it for the headlines.

Online, there are stills of them, hanging out in the background among the best boys and gaffers and makeup artists. In their paisley and buckskin, they're conspicuous in retrospect only because you know what to look for. They grin and watch her, planning what they'll do, how they'll come for her when she's alone, when her beau is away shooting another movie in Paris.

And there she is, standing nearby, blissful and ignorant, smiling at the man she already considered her husband, while

182

he's smiling at a pretty redheaded extra who blushes and smiles back.

You try not to think of any of that. You try to focus on her.

Every night for a week, the film plays on repeat in your apartment. Your friends text you and invite you out for drinks or a movie, but you don't text back. Anyhow, you already have a movie, and it's better than anything they could offer. On the fifth night, your girlfriend calls and chastises you for standing her up at dinner. You don't remember having a girlfriend, but she sounds vexed enough that you take her at her word about it and apologize.

"Maybe sometime next week?" you say, and hang up.

On the television, the film is frozen. You reach for the remote, but she trembles on the screen, and you realize the movie isn't paused. *She's* paused, reclined on a chaise lounge, not moving, not speaking, her long legs tucked under her, as though she's waiting on you.

"Sorry," you say, and power down your phone. No more distractions. This is where you want to be, here with her. Your time together seems more real than your time with still-living people. If any of them are really living.

She drifts back to her role of an ill-fated model, and you blink at the glare of the screen. All the lights in the apartment are off. You don't remember turning them off, but you must have.

The final frame of the film soft-focuses on her face. She smiles at something off-camera, but it's a strained smile, a practiced smile, one coaxed from her by a patient director.

She glances at you, and her skin glistens like the ocean at dawn, but she doesn't reach for you.

Then the screen fades to black, and she's gone, that smile is gone, and you're alone.

In the dark of your apartment, you wonder about the last time she smiled for real. There must have been a last time, even if she hadn't known it then, hadn't known the hyenas were coming, were already on their way to slit the screen in her Malibu house and orchestrate her third act.

You wonder what made her smile that final time. A sunset maybe, or a silly joke, or something secret, something that belonged to only her.

You wonder if it even matters.

You're sure it does.

The fifth film isn't a film at all. Not unless you count snuff as a genre.

In it, she begs for her life. Two full minutes of pleas and bargaining, and then just quiet sobs before the flash of a knife in the lens. Before the world crumbles to black.

This film is the easiest of the five to locate. You can sit down at your computer any day and find it there. YouTube has removed the clip a thousand times, but somebody somewhere will upload it again, and the cycle will start over. If people want something, you can't stop them from getting it. Death has an impeccable retail value.

So you join the fifty million previous viewers, and press play. Her voice is scratchy and wheezing and not like her, though no one would claim this one is dubbed. Thirty seconds in, you wince and turn away, but you force yourself to look back, to live this moment with her. You can't abandon her, not now, not when she needs you most. You might not be able to help her, but at least you won't leave her alone.

In the sidebars of the screen under *Up Next*, there might be another video of her from happier times, on a nothing talk show in a sparkling Lycra dress, or in a behind-the-scenes documentary waving at the camera in a puffy jacket, her breath fogging around her face like smoke on a cold early morning shoot. There will also be videos of her hyena-grunting killers, interviews after their arrest, after their skipping into the courtroom like schoolchildren on a fieldtrip, after they settled down years later and learned a little something about regret.

There will always be more videos of them than her. They're the real stars. Before the verdict of guilty on all counts was ever read, true-crime books about them had already crawled to the tops of bestseller lists, and TV movies based on their bloody exploits were nominated for Emmys and Golden Globes. And when the usual monster angle gets stale, fresh-faced California writers will recast them as misunderstood, as Byronic, as just like us.

No one will want to tell her story. This is a truth no one openly admits—that murderers are always more interesting than victims.

Victims are tally marks, case files to be completed and cataloged and tucked away in dusty file cabinets.

Victims are someone to blame.

If only she'd locked the door and closed all the windows.

If only she'd screamed as loudly as she did in her films.

If only she'd been stronger and fought back.

If only, if only, if only.

Because the dead-and-buried generate few headlines, the world forgets her, slowly at first, and then almost altogether. She becomes an obscure trivia question, the kind in a final tournament round that wins a league team twenty-five dollars in buffalo wing vouchers.

She becomes an entry in an online encyclopedia that starts with her death and then maybe mentions her career, her childhood, her life. Maybe.

She becomes a cipher. A ghost, but not a ghost, because at least a ghost exists in the white noises and the shadows. These days, she hardly gets that.

The hyenas fare better. They snicker and enjoy conjugal

visits and find God in prison, as if He's hiding in the corner of their cell behind the toilet, like mildew or a cockroach.

In interviews televised during primetime with smiley blonde reporters who boast more hair than heart, the hyenas clean up well, and they even say they're sorry.

But hyenas lie.

❧

Perhaps we lied, too. Perhaps there's a sixth film, if you're brave enough to search for it.

Prepare yourself, though, because this one won't be easy to find. It never hit Netflix or YouTube. Even most bootleggers claim it doesn't exist.

"An urban legend," they'll tell you when you ask.

But they're wrong.

It's out there, and if you're patient, if you comb all the film convention tables and seedy backrooms at dying video stores, you'll find it. A VHS cassette with her name written on the spine. It comes with a warning label, the type a character in a horror film would ignore and then wish he hadn't.

You aren't like that character. You already know the risks.

You don't care.

Even once you unearth the video, it takes you another week to dig up a VCR. You finally buy one at a yard sale for ten dollars too much. The curmudgeonly old couple with matching gray hair can see how much you want it, and they refuse to give you a deal. Most of the buttons are worn off, and the tracking on the tape is a mess, but it doesn't matter. Once she materializes among the static, everything else falls away.

Her body flickering with life and promise, she tips up her chin beneath a spotlight, and you realize it: she's there waiting for you. She's always been waiting for you. Even before there was a you to wait for.

And you've been waiting for her.

You move toward the television, so close you fog up the screen. On the other side, her breath does the same.

"Thank you for coming," she'll say, and it will be her voice, all of her voices, the ones they trained and the ones she trained herself. "Are you ready for my final performance?"

"Yes," you'll say, and mean it.

Overhead, the lights flicker, and the apartment wobbles around you. With the weight of the sky pressing into your bones, she smiles, a real smile, a smile that glows and twists and lights up the universe. A smile that sears all the bad in the world and turns it to dust. Outside, glass shatters, and brick facades crumble, and your apartment disintegrates to cinders around you. The blazing world smells of smoke and lies and the pelts of feral animals who tried to steal the world, animals who did their best to strip her of everything she was—her body, her voice, her life.

But even in death, she's more alive than they ever were, and she doesn't belong to them, not anymore. They belong to her, and she reduces them to ash with the rest.

You toss your head back and laugh, because you're glad to see it all smolder. She'll laugh too, and as the edges of your life singe away, she'll reach through the screen. Still smiling, she'll pull you out of the world that tried so hard to obliterate her, a world that failed because at least you remembered her. And now with no world to go back to, she remembers you.

In a Technicolor haze of her own making, she'll hold you close, and you'll hold her.

And in the final frame, as the universe fades to black, you'll save each other.

THE
LAZARUS
BRIDE

W E END IN fire. All beautiful things end in fire.

❧

It's midnight when you slip from the satin sheets of our honeymoon bed, the train of your wedding gown stalking behind you. In your wake, the room smells of yesterday's church ceremony, like stale buttercream icing and Bible verses we didn't believe.

I sit up on the cold mattress and watch you through the picture window. Outside, the summer air shimmers, and you wander barefoot along the front lawn of our rented cottage, your body a senseless shape in a world of shadows.

You look back once, your heavy gaze the color of the ivy creeping over the trees. I almost call to you through the glass, but my lips tremble, and I think better of it.

Right now, you want to be alone. The gold band on my ring finger itches, and I wait for you to return to me.

189

I wait too long.

The glow is faint at first, so dim and distorted that not until the flames have cascaded down the curves of your thighs, your waist, your breasts, do I realize you're burning.

I blink back in the light, convinced it's a mirage or a fever dream. But this is no illusion. The blaze dances and coils and climbs higher into the sky, and handfuls of your skin melt into neat, colorless puddles like silver dollar pancakes.

Someone is screaming. I'm screaming. I'm screaming and stumbling and trying to reach the door, trying to reach you, but it's too late.

You close what's left of your eyes, and your body turns to ash.

※

We met in ice. It was the dawn of December two years ago, and you were showing your art at a gallery downtown. Friends of friends had told me about you. You crafted weird mixed media on giant canvases, using images of willowy models clipped from vintage issues of *Harper's Bazaar* and *Vogue*. With a sheen of Mod Podge, you pasted them back together, so that their bodies were disjointed, hips a mosaic of odd angles and mismatched eyes too big and too small at the same time. Fabulous stuff, the critics said, award-winning stuff, strange stuff that I never quite understood, though I pretended to.

Everyone knew you then, the cool girl with the stop-sign red lips and the scuffed Doc Martens you salvaged from a thrift store. You frequented all the best warehouse parties and cocktail bars and hip little coffeehouses where the playlists alternated between Modest Mussorgsky and sad-sack emo boys crooning over lost love.

The gallery should have been packed with your admirers that night, cooing over your latest installation of jumbled girls, but a storm descended, and with the frozen roads diamond-slick, nobody braved the weather except me. So you had to make do with one admirer.

"Thank you for coming," you said when you realized that I'd won your attention by default. "My name's Gillian."

"I'm Terence." I choked on my own name. I wasn't there to meet you. I wanted to meet you, of course, but I also wanted to blend in with the plaster, to disappear in plain sight. I was there for the art. That was what I told myself. But I was really there for you.

The sleet pelted the windows like fists, and we drank martinis—enough for a dozen invisible guests—and we talked about anarchy and politics and Picasso's Blue Period. A lump in my chest swelled, and I scavenged like a vulture through every tidbit of Art History trivia from my freshman year course a decade ago. You outfoxed me by a mile, and you grinned over the rim of your cocktail glass, because you knew it. You knew I was struggling, that I was desperate to impress you. Everything about me amused you, from the yellow tweed print of my jacket to the name of my job.

"A switchman?" you asked with a giggle. "It sounds like you're detonating a bomb."

After the storm withered away and the gallery lights dimmed, you asked me to meet you the next night at the ice rink on North Shore. I was sure that it was a cruel prank, that I would wait for you in vain for hours. But when I arrived, bundled up with my breath fogging around me like smoke, you were already there, two pairs of rented ice skates in hand.

"I figured you were about a size ten." You smiled. "Is that right?"

I nodded, and together, we slid into our bladed boots. Our legs quivering, you laced your fingers with mine and guided me onto the ice. I couldn't skate and neither could you, but that didn't matter. We crashed into each other exceptionally well, our prickled skin and flimsy bones wrapped together in a never-ending fall.

"Isn't this fun?" you asked as we peeled our bruised bodies from the ice.

"Yes," I said, my voice a wisp of air, breathless with chill and wanting you.

We fell again and again in the cold, and it was all a great game to you. Your laugh was wind-chime clear, and when you kissed me, your lips tasted like sugar and ice and light, something pure and indecipherable.

You had no place of your own, just a loan on a friend's Cabernet-stained futon, so you invited yourself to my house for the night. In the dim of my bedroom, you undressed me, your fingers flicking open each button on my shirt like you were taunting me, like any moment you might laugh and leave me alone. But you didn't leave. You unzipped your dress and crawled in bed next to me. I held you as close as I could without smothering you. Your body wrapped around mine, and you were so alive you practically glowed, your skin pale as a phantom in the moonlight.

I should have known then you weren't supposed to last.

✺✺

Your body is burned now, everything reduced to ash except that golden symbol of eternity I bought for you, the one that never quite fit your narrow finger.

A mesh of red maples reaches overhead like hands united in prayer, and the leaves are the color of fresh blood, alive and new and dew-draped. This is the lustrous heart of summer, but we welcome no pink moon, no fireflies, no shrill call of the cicada. Not a speck of life dwells in this place, not even you.

My hands search the detritus for a sign of you, for a patch of unburned skin or the scorched socket of a hip joint. But you're not here. Where you've gone I cannot fathom, so I shape the cinders into an effigy of you. Your face, your waist, your long legs. This is the closest I can get.

I tip my head to the sky, my cheeks dripping with char-black tears, and I say your name, over and over in its every permutation. Murmuring it like a prayer, shrieking it like a curse, enunciating it with an even tongue as though I'm a preacher reading off a list of the dead.

I say it a thousand times until the word loses its meaning, until the sound boils in my ears and makes my lips go numb. Somehow, this is enough. Piece by piece, your body reconstitutes, skin and bone and hair emerging from the void.

The ash remembers. Even your wedding dress returns unblemished.

You are whole again, and you inhale a breath, your first breath back from the grave.

"Gillian?" I whisper the word this time, not quite believing it.

Your lips part, and your voice is so slight it barely disturbs the air. "Terence?"

Relief, potent as absinthe, surges through my chest. Sobbing, I take you into my arms and carry you inside to the claw-foot tub where I run a cold bath, the coldest bath I can, enough to overwhelm the echo of the flames that stole you from me. A fresh bar of lavender soap scrubs the soot from your skin, and here you are, as beautiful and gleaming as the night we met. I wrap you in a Jacquard-woven towel and escort you to the bed.

"How did it happen?" I ask, my hands entwined with yours.

You shake your head, and I let it pass. I won't pry too deep and break this spell. You've come back to me, and that's all I could want.

In the slanting golden light of afternoon, we make love, our first time as husband and wife. Your back arches, and you shiver in my arms, moaning once. It's a cry of pleasure, I assume, of gratefulness for how I saved you, how I coaxed you back from nothingness.

Our naked limbs curve together in a half moon, and we fall asleep.

For hours, I dream of disjointed women likes the ones on your canvases, and I dream of words too, of a mantra panted with avid desperation. *You're mine, you're mine, I won't let you go or wither or burn, I'll save you. I'll protect you.*

But I can't protect you, not from yourself.

I awaken alone at midnight in a snarl of still-damp sheets, the stench of barbequed flesh creeping through the stone façade of the cottage. You're outside again and already alight. My feet a tangle of briars beneath me, I stagger from the bedroom, but like last night, I cannot reach you in time.

The last flames die out, and I collapse on the lawn. You're ash and smoke and sorrow in my arms. It's in this moment that I understand your moan in bed was not grateful.

It was nothing more than a death rattle.

⁜

After our first date on the ice, you were my own personal ghost—in my bed one evening and gone for weeks after. A bohemian lifestyle, you called it, but whenever you'd turn up at my door in the middle of the night, I knew it was because the overpriced hostel kicked you out for nonpayment, or you woke up on your friend's futon after a party to discover a strange man pawing at you.

"Do you ever plan on finding somewhere you can settle down?" I tried not to sound too hopeful, tried not to let on that I wanted you there with me, in my house, in my bed.

"Maybe someday."

You curled into me and closed your eyes. Tucked against my chest, you looked unreal, a meteor in the night that flares and dissipates. In the dark, I liked to tether myself to you, two fingers coiled around your wrist or the palm of my hand on your bare thigh. Anything to connect my body to yours, to bind us together, to keep you from disappearing like melted snow in spring.

You opened your eyes and smiled. "The way you hold me," you said, your gaze bright as wildfire, "it's like I'm falling, but you've already caught me."

"Always," I said, and pressed my fingers a little deeper into your flesh until I felt the gentle throb in your veins.

We went to warehouse parties together, and gallery openings that weren't in ice storms, ones that were well attended with people who trilled your name and bought up your work like you'd never decorate another canvas. Everywhere we went, I lagged behind you like a lost child. You were the star, and I was the shadow.

I never knew why you picked me. You could have had anybody. All the boys salivated after you, but you shooed them off like they were red ants invading a summer picnic.

"Nuisances," you said, and pulled me closer. "I don't want them. I want you."

You kissed me, and everything cascaded away except the two of us.

We were dating three months when I took you home to meet my family. Everybody loved you. Even my mother, who never liked my girlfriends, especially the pretty ones, pinched my arm after dinner and whispered, "Hold on to that one. She's a keeper."

It was Easter Sunday. On the television, a fluffy-headed Moses parted the Red Sea, and at the table, my father won his third straight game of Scrabble. You laughed and blushed and said all the right things, and by the time my mother covered the leftover scalloped potatoes in tin foil and waved goodbye to us at the back door, I loved you so much it made my stomach whirl.

Halfway home on the highway, I gripped the wheel tighter. "Did you have a nice time?" I asked stupidly, because I could think of nothing else to say.

You smiled, and took my hand. "You're everything I thought you were," you said, and I didn't know if that was a compliment or an insult. Perhaps I was too normal for you, too banal, or maybe that was what you liked about me, how different I was from you. Maybe that was why you picked me.

I bit down hard to keep myself from asking, but the question escaped my lips anyhow. "Would you like to move in with me?"

You hesitated, the word thick as honey on your tongue.

"Yes," you said.

It was the first time you ever lied to me.

⁂

I can never reach you before you burn, but I can always coax you back. You've retreated to ash a thousand times now, and I've saved you from the void each night, but it's never enough.

The leaves overhead are red and new. It is always summer here, and it is always our honeymoon. A wedding night that never ends. We live this day over and over.

"Until we get it right," you say, and I hate you a little for it, I hate you for suggesting that what I've done isn't right. Should I bury your remains and leave you to the afterlife? How is that love?

The midnight blaze disintegrates you faster each time, so that even when I'm looking right at you, I've never seen you strike a match. I've searched the property—every closet, every corner—for the gasoline that ignites you, but nothing's here.

Again tonight, you burn anew, brilliant and luscious, your

flames the color of a ripe tangerine. I run to you, and when I don't make it, I sob, as though this is the first time I've lost you. It always feels like the first time.

My throat raw, I call out your name, and you return.

In the chilled bathwater, your fingers prune, and the leftover ash swirls like a vortex around you. I massage the lavender soap into your belly, and the skin reddens and chafes.

"Why are you doing this?" I gag up the words, and my hands go numb, but I scrub on, polishing away the remnants of your soot and self-hatred.

"Because I can't help it."

You dry your hair and slide back into your wedding dress. Although you brought a dozen frocks and tank tops and high-waisted shorts, you wear nothing except the gown that reminds me of regret.

I track you through the house, your silhouette always a half-step ahead of me. "Let's go to the general store today."

"Why?" You're in the kitchen on your tiptoes, reaching into the tallest cupboard.

I lean against the doorway to steady my shaking. "Maybe someone there could help us."

You laugh, and the sharp, sad sound is like a dying night-ingale. "Fine."

Before we leave, you pull six bags of black tea from the top shelf and drop them into a pitcher filled with slightly yellowed water from the faucet.

I lock the front door behind us, and you set the pitcher on the front step in the sun.

The only trail out of here curves into a forest canopy, and the deep mud of the path seeps up around your satin heels and squishes beneath your toes.

You shake your head and sigh. "We don't belong here."

My stomach twists. This wasn't your choice for a honey-moon. You would have preferred Madrid or Paris or even the kitsch charm of Niagara Falls. But I wanted somewhere for us to escape, somewhere for us to be together, just you and me, so I booked us the remotest cabin I could find, a place with one Greyhound stop and no other way in or out. The bus won't return for a week, and since tomorrow never comes here, we're stranded.

We leave thick footprints behind us as we wind around the trail into a clearing. Below, our cottage sits drowsing in a distant hollow.

I stare down at it. "It looks so strange from faraway."

"Everything is different with distance," you say, and keep moving.

Around a sharp bend, the general store comes into view. This is the only place within a day's walk, the sole fragment of civilization we can reach before you burn again. The rusted bell over the door jingles, and a ring of grim-faced men glances up lazily at us as we shuffle inside. We've come here a hundred times already, trying to find a way out, but these men never seem to remember us. Perhaps they remember nothing at all. Maybe their days here have always been identical, an indistinguishable blur of nothing conversation and runny tobacco juice spat into old Coca-Cola bottles.

You disappear down an aisle filled with bulk herbs, dried and neatly packaged. The sweep of your dress curls behind you like the photonegative of a shadow.

One of the men squints after you. "Newlyweds, huh?"

I nod, though it's no longer true. You and I have spent years as a married couple now. Years, or only one night.

I gnaw the inside of my cheek and ask the same question I always ask. "Could we get a ride out of here?"

The man behind the counter whistles. "Sorry," he says, his lips bunched up in the shape of a distorted rosebud. "Truck's broken down."

Another man grunts. "All the trucks are broken down."

I heave in, and the air tastes of nicotine and abandoned dreams. "Do you maybe have a phone then?"

"Nope, son. Sorry about that."

My stomach twists again. This is the answer I expect, but it always hurts, the hopelessness of this place, how we've gotten ourselves in but can't get out again.

You purchase an ounce of cloves and lavender flowers, and pay for them in loose change.

"Thank you," you say to the men, and they brighten and watch us leave, a longing in their eyes. Maybe you're the reflection of the girl they loved once, the girl that slipped away from them, the one they can't forget.

Outside the store, you take my hand, and we walk back in silence.

At the cottage, the sun has warmed the pitcher and made us tea for the afternoon.

❧

When you moved in, you brought almost nothing with you, just a paisley hand-me-down suitcase stuffed with secondhand dresses and silly keepsakes. A locket with no key or photo or secret inside. Your first paintbrush, too withered and tangled and loved to use again. A picture of a woman, your mother probably, though when I asked you once who she was, you shrugged and said, "Nobody." I never asked again.

We eschewed the fancy parties and the cocktail bars, and stayed in to make Thai food and watch reruns of *I Love Lucy* and *Burns and Allen*. You never complained. This was a nice life, a sturdy life, with no pawing guests and space enough for you to work. I was sure this was what you wanted.

You set up in the spare bedroom at a canvas half the size of the wall. From the kitchen, I heard the rustling of magazines and the snick-snack of scissors disassembling the glossy pages, but whenever I peeked in at you, you covered the canvas with a king-sized white sheet.

"How's your next show coming?" I asked.

"Okay," you said without inflection. Another lie.

I decided you needed the house to feel like your own. So I hired a contractor who tore the wallpaper from every room and slathered paint in the palette you requested. Lemon yellows and burgundies and apricots.

"Anything you want," I said, "it's yours."

"Thank you." You pulled me close and kissed me, and for a moment, I tasted ice. I tasted our first date, our joy, our past. I'm sure you tasted it, too.

But it didn't help. Your work remained stalled, and sometimes, in the middle of the night, I would stir from bed and discover you wandering through the gaping doorways of the house, like a specter without chains, without anything to weigh you down and steady you in this unfamiliar place.

"What can I do?" I asked, but you just shook your head.

There was no reason for you to be unhappy. You had everything a person could desire. This should have been enough. But I could have proffered you a kingdom and still not made you smile.

Most nights, I cooked alone, burning curries and oversteaming rice and staring at your plate, sullen and cold, across the dinner table.

Sometimes, you joined me. Those nights were almost worse, the two of us chewing our overdone steak and sipping our boxed Zinfandel and wishing we could cut through the silence that clotted thick as mud between us.

"Our life isn't so bad," I said one evening. "There are other women who would be grateful for this."

Instantly, I wanted to reach into the space between us and crush the words from existence. But it was too late. With you, I was always too late.

You speared a sprig of wilted asparagus and said nothing. You didn't speak through the rest of dinner, or afterwards. In bed that night, you turned away from me, your body smoldering to the touch, the comforter kicked to the floor. It wasn't until the next morning over thin coffee and thinner conversation that you met my gaze, your wildfire eyes dull and distant.

"If you're not happy," you said, "why don't you find yourself one of those other women and leave me alone?"

You could have slit open my eye with a razor and hurt me less.

"I *am* happy," I said.

We didn't speak again for three days. At last, I came into your room where you stared at the sheet tugged over the canvas.

"I'm sorry," I said.

"So am I." Your hands quivering, you reached toward me as if I wasn't real, as if I were a stranger. Then you unfastened my shirt, one button at a time, not teasing now, but with a hand that could do nothing else, a hand desperate to remember. This was our only way to solve anything. Your every touch became an apology. So did mine.

Afterwards, you curled into me, and I pretended it would be okay. I could fix us. I could fix you. But all I could manage was to bury us deeper into this life.

On our anniversary, I kneeled before you with a black velvet box and a ring that cost six months' salary.

"Sure," you said without looking at me. "I'll marry you."

❧

We sit together on the front step of the cottage and sip sun tea from smudged glasses.

"It wasn't supposed to be this way." You gulp down another heavy mouthful of dark liquid. "We were better off before we met."

201

"Maybe," I say, and despise myself for admitting it. "But now I can't be happy without you."

You exhale a rueful laugh. "That's the trick of love, isn't it?"

You say nothing else, but it's easy to guess what you mean. The trick is how love rearranges your life, how it cleaves you in two, so that there's the before and there's the after, two halves irreconcilable from the other. Your new life becomes something you can no longer recognize, but your old life is gone too.

And in this forgotten land far from home, we have nothing except each other. Not that we even have that.

The gossamer edges of night creep closer like long tendrils of smoke.

I clutch my glass so tight it warps in my hand. "I love you."

"I love you too," you say, but the melancholy in your voice says that's not always enough.

I close my eyes and breathe in the scents of lace and leaves and earth.

Tonight will be different.

Tonight, this will end.

❦

We would be happy. That was what I promised myself. Down to the last square of white lace, I planned us a fairy tale wedding, forgetting that some fairy tales end with armless girls and eyes pecked out by hungry crows.

Before we left home for the chapel, I sneaked into the spare room where you kept your canvas. You were already in the car, so with a careful hand, I peeled back the white sheet. My chest tightened, and the world spiraled around me like a broken top. The figures no longer had large eyes and jagged hips. They no longer looked like girls at all. They were gaunt towers, misshapen and vile, like pillars of salt scorched with flames.

Grimacing, I turned away and locked the door behind me.

At a pristine altar, we said our vows and our "I do's," and I removed your veil to reveal a face I hardly recognized. It didn't matter. I kissed you anyhow. A kiss would be enough, I told myself, so long as it was real, so long as I meant it. Love breaks the spell, after all. It transforms the beast back into royalty. It coaxes the apple-poisoned princess from her coffin of glass and slumber. Love would be enough. It had to be enough.

At the reception, you did not blush or smile or dine on a slice of red velvet cake, a flavor that I thought was your favorite. You didn't dance either, not even when the DJ spun every sappy song for inspiration.

"Too tired," you said, and I huddled beside you holding your hand as the guests imbibed and caroused and wished us all the best.

But there would be no best, no good tidings, no happily ever after. With your veil tucked behind your ears, you vanished before my eyes, retreating into the places I could not reach you, into a darkness as encompassing as death itself. And no one could sense it but me. All they saw was a bride in an unspoiled dress who tipped up her chin and tossed her bouquet and clapped for the unlucky girl who caught it.

One by one, the pink-faced guests departed, leftover cake tucked in bow-wrapped favor boxes under their arms. We waved goodbye to them and pretended not to sense the weight of our mistake bearing down on us like a thousand quarry stones.

The midnight tickets quivered in my hand as I slung our luggage over my shoulder. "The bus will be here soon. Don't you want to change?"

"I'm fine," you said, and fidgeted in your lace and satin, the seams clenched in your hands like a nervous child at Sunday school.

I didn't argue. There was nothing left for us to say.

When the wheezing bus arrived, I clasped your hand and helped you up the stairs, and together, we took the long ride to eternity.

⚜

I wake in the dark. The iced tea pitcher is empty, and I'm alone. On the step next to me, you left behind your glass, a red kiss imprinted on the rim.

A humid gust swallows me up, and I know beyond reason, it's almost midnight. Our last midnight.

At the edges of the lawn, you wander, your body already glowing with a preternatural warmth. My bones heavy beneath my flesh, I go to you. Nothing stops me this time. That's because I've finally realized it. I can't save you. I can't protect you.

But I can join you.

The flames rise from your body, and though it aches to touch you, I wrap both hands around your waist.

You gape at me, the tips of your hair curling and shriveling away. "Don't do this," you whisper.

"It's okay." I entwine your fingers with mine, and the palms of my hands turn to black, but I won't let you go.

I'll sway at your side and burn with you. This will be our first dance together. Our first and our last, a lifetime suspended in a moment. A marriage not built to survive a day.

The reek of seared flesh—yours and mine, though mostly yours—lilts around us, and you wither in my arms, growing smaller and smaller, the ash of you falling through the air like dried rice tossed at a happy couple.

My lips part, but no scream comes out, only an echo of grief. I want to take it all back—the wedding, the house, our bitter-cold first kiss. I want to tell you how sorry I am. But more than anything, I want to stay here with you, in this unchanging summer, in this unchanging place. I want to hold you tighter than life itself, but I can't hold you at all. You've already turned to dust in my arms.

Though my skin smokes, I never dissolve into nothing. I'm not like you. Your body smolders from the inside out. This fire is meant for you alone.

When the last flames wink out, I lay the soft shape of you on the blackened pyre, as if this is our wedding bed. In a way, it is and always will be.

"I love you," I say, and I mean it with every iota of my soul, but it no longer matters.

I've been wrong.

You can't tame fire. You can try to contain it, or you can smother it altogether, but either way, you deny it, you deny the essence of what makes it fire, what makes it wild, what makes us love the things we can't control.

I wait with you a long time, without sobbing, without speaking your name, without moving at all.

Bit by bit, you emerge. I am not coaxing you from the ash. This is your doing. And this time, you're different. The wedding gown has melted away, and your naked body is a blank canvas ripe for a fresh start.

I won't wait for you to awaken. I won't beg your forgiveness or ask for us to start again. For the first time, I'll make the right choice.

Your diamond lies next to you in the grass. I slip off my own gold band, and it falls alongside your ring. Then, with steady fingers, I drop a handful of dirt over our promises, and the earth devours them.

I leave everything behind—my ring, my bag, my bride— and head down the sinuous path that led us here. The bus might come early today, or the men at the general store will have fixed their trucks. Someone or something will take me away from here. I'll be stranded no longer. And when you're ready, you won't be stranded either. You will go wherever you desire. Far from me.

Along the trail, I pass the outlines of yesterday's footprints, a reminder that we were here, we were together. It was real, you and me, even if it couldn't last.

I pass through the trees and crest into a clearing.

My heart a pillar of salt, I look back once.

Overnight, the tips of the leaves have turned golden, and an eager chill whips through the air. Autumn will come now. Though I wanted to stop it, tomorrow has come.

Below, your body is fully formed. Your chest rises and falls like the tides, and you breathe again. You breathe easy. You breathe without me.

I breathe without you, too. I wish I couldn't, but this is the way it was meant to be. I whisper once more that I love you and then I whisper goodbye. Smiling, I turn away and move into the first glint of sunrise.

Behind me, summer ends, and you open your eyes.

Gwendolyn Kiste is a speculative fiction author based in Pennsylvania. Her work has appeared in *Nightmare, Shimmer, Interzone, Three-Lobed Burning Eye,* and *LampLight,* as well as Flame Tree Publishing's *Chilling Horror Short Stories,* among others.

A native of Ohio, she currently dwells on an abandoned horse farm outside of Pittsburgh with her husband, two cats, and not nearly enough ghosts. You can find her online at gwendolynkiste.com.

CPSIA information can be obtained
at www.ICGtesting.com
Printed in the USA
BVHW041412280423
663226BV00001B/178